TABLE OF CONTENTS

D.R. HILL – A SHORT BIOGRAPHY

D.R. Hill is originally from Birmingham, UK and has an Honours Degree from the University of Hull and an MA in Acting from the University of Essex. He has worked as a theatre and arts practitioner and manager. Previous publications include *Under Scan* (co-written with Rafael Lozano-Hemmer), *Voices of Culture* (*The Role of Culture in Promoting Refugee Inclusion*) co-written as a commission from the European Union, and *ArtReach – 25 Years of Cultural Development*. His short stories '3250' and 'House Clearance' have both been published by Bandit Fiction and in 2021 he was shortlisted for a second time for Eyelands International Book Awards, this time for his novel, *From Now On*. He has also had plays performed by Theatre Station Blyth and Everyman Theatre, Cheltenham and co-wrote *Peace in Our Town* with Barrie Keeffe. He is married with two sons and lives in Berkshire.

HOUSE CLEARANCE

SHORT STORIES BY

D. R. HILL

COLLECTION SHORTLISTED FOR
THE EYELANDS INTERNATIONAL
BOOK AWARDS 2019

Dixon and Galt LLP

House Clearance
Copyright © 2022 by D.R. Hill All rights reserved.
First Edition: 2022

Paperback ISBN: 978-1-7396863-1-4
Hardcover ISBN: 978-1-7396863-4-5
Ebook ISBN: 978-1-7396863-5-2

Published by:

Dixon and Galt LLP

ACKNOWLEDGEMENTS

Thanks to Martha Sprackland for advice on these stories, and to Streetlight Graphics for the design.

Quoted lines from *I Can See for Miles* in 'The Boarder', courtesy of Pete Townsend and Spirit Music Group

This book is dedicated to Evelyn Harrison

THE MAN WHO CHANGED HIS FACE

Day One

HE'D FORGOTTEN ABOUT THE TUNNEL just before the station. The train whined as it slowed down and, standing prematurely, he was caught in the dark and momentarily thrown off balance.

The train was old, the door opening from an outside handle, so that stepping down onto the tired concrete platform seemed like a step back in time. However, the station had been painted: garishly, without thought. The original, subtle, heritage hues had been covered over, though underneath the station was the same. Only the colours were different. They created a plastic-looking façade, mocking the originality that had been lost.

He was the last to leave the platform, and relished being alone. The solid, splintery, wooden steps up over the footbridge were untarnished, the ground beneath his feet the same as he remembered it.

He came out onto the station forecourt and clocked the weighbridge office now bricked up and silent. The sun came from behind clouds but an unexpected chill ran through him. On the side wall of Liddecomb's the original penny farthing, hoisted high and fastened, still held its place, but it was no longer a bicycle shop. On the street-front, bouquets, baskets and bunches of spring flowers now competed with wreaths and roses in an extravagant front of house display to rival a festival show; or the heaps of flora at a crematorium. Other than the penny farthing, not another bicycle in sight.

And still the old library building looked unoccupied. He hurried past, not anxious to take the turning to the location that was the primary reason for his return. However, walking on down the Old High Street was not aimless. He was heading in the direction of the mill, and the river, and the backwater where the sound of the flow streaming through the sluice would soon be heard.

But he didn't hear it.

The mill was closed. Boarded up, unused, the public footpaths that wound through its outbuildings and perimeter overgrown, a silent place, like a churchyard. And where was the sound of the sluice?

Then the backwater was visible, the diversion of the river and the tumbling cascade he remembered that churned the pool below. But today that was still, barely a trickle spinning over the edge, the controlling gates of the sluice rusted.

The high, concrete dam was fenced, restricting access. From the footpath it was possible to coax the brambles aside and squeeze through to the water's edge. There the pond slapped gently against the bank, a nonchalant, harmless gesture. The water was dark and oily though, untroubled by serious disturbance. This was no place to swim. It was abandoned, like toxic waste.

Back on the Old High Street he found the Bluebell suspiciously welcoming.

'You'll want an en-suite… Business is booming in these parts so you're lucky it's a holiday week. Most people book ahead. No car?' He booked for six nights.

Ordering a bottle of wine for one he felt looked inappropriate, might attract attention, so in the end he settled for a large carafe. It was inexplicable that the bar offered "specials", including freshly baked pike, when the customer base appeared to be two regular drinkers on bar stools sinking slow pints. In his corner of the bar he addressed himself to the issue of supper, whilst observing the sexy barmaid-cum-waitress, possibly landlady, warmly deflecting the occasional double-entendre and uninspiring chit chat. In perfect time she came over to take his order.

'You're here in a holiday week. We normally have regular business clients. They entertain. The quaintness here is seen as attractive. But you're right, I doubt we'll serve many portions of pike tonight!'

He settled for a more mundane dish and was curious. She was educated, attractive, and surely not tied to the landlord, the paunchy and bluff host who had shown him to a room.

'I only work here,' she told him, between courses. 'It's very convenient and I quite like doing shifts… it's not exactly hard work! But whatever brings you here?'

What brings you here… he would have resisted the question if it had been asked by the host, or the regulars at the bar. But he melted.

'I've come to see my mother,' he said. Her expression barely flickered but he could tell she had ticker-taped the information and drawn a number of inferences and question marks. He could also tell she knew not to ask more. 'I've not been here… for a while,' he added.

Outside the moon was bright, full or nearly so. With some courage from the carafe, he retraced his steps back towards the station and took that familiar turn. The street yawned down below. He was conscious of his footsteps hitting the silence of the evening. There were no lights in the windows of his mother's house. As he paused briefly outside a curtain moved next door, and he had a momentary glimpse of a male face framed within a small pane of glass, apparently staring out into the street, seeing him. Then the curtain was drawn, the faint light was extinguished and the face was gone.

Day Two

When he woke up, he knew that the only way to go through with it was not to think.

His friend from last night, Joanne, served breakfast. Despite the tightness in his abdomen he lingered over the food, stimulated by the snatches of conversation and glad of the chance to pass time in company. All his senses felt heightened.

'Did you know we have an operating cinema here now?' she told him. 'The building's been taken over by a Trust, so we get interesting films, not just the mainstream. It's been fully restored.'

He mentioned he had recently been to Cannes. 'But I'm not in the industry, at least not directly.'

She revealed she had been, was, an actress. 'But it's hard to get work now, my age is difficult – not young and fresh, but not quite old enough.' She laughed and revealed more. He had misjudged from her appearance and had to make a swift recalculation. She was only seven years younger than him.

Back in his room he studied his face, and wondered how different it looked if not seen through the mirror, in reverse. How recognisable was he? With a tie the suit looked too formal. He might be a financial advisor seeking to maximise the benefits of pension arrangements. Well, he *was* a financial advisor, of sorts. He laughed to himself. Without the tie he felt there was an air of flippancy, a casualness that failed to match and acknowledge the occasion. He went with the tie.

Joanne shouted after him from the break-bar-reception, half-jokingly, 'Have a nice day.'

As he turned the corner by the old library the effort not to think was screaming in his head. Words that were neutral and acceptable repeated themselves in ever-faster combination. A group of small children, with bikes and tricycles, were playing in the old library car park. He remembered his own first bicycle. The children were laying out cones and bricks to reproduce a small-town Le Mans. He paused, to watch and momentarily delay the inevitability of his visit, jealous of their easy focus and innocence.

And then he was at the door. It was shabby, a repaint needed, the doorbell loose on the doorframe, the ring unpredictable, noiseless. Was it working? He knocked loudly on the door, before he lost his nerve, and almost immediately it was opened.

The woman who stood in the doorway looked puzzled. He noticed the loss of weight. It gave her a shocking, lined appearance beyond her age. She would now be seventy-four. He could sense a frailness which was unexpected. It did not match the personality he remembered. She was supported by two sticks. Her puzzlement changed to wonder, then to flecks of anger, resentment. Finally, she spoke.

'You've come back.'

He didn't know what to say.

'You'd better come in.'

She stood aside to let him through into the not-as-familiar hall-way. It smelt odd. He noticed her careful glance into the street to see whether his arrival had been noticed.

'Go through to the back room.'

He walked on ahead. Despite the spring sun peeping through the window she had the electric fire on. Through the back door he could see that the steps and paths were covered in moss, and that the white, wrought-iron gate leading to next door, and then to the entry, and that he had painted as a teenager, was flaking and dirty. She came into the room.

'I'm not going to kiss you.' Before he could respond she went on. 'It hurts, moving my head and neck. I have MS. That's why I have these sticks.' She dropped into a chair.

'I'm sorry,' he replied.

She looked up sharply and said, 'What for?'

He looked away, into the garden.

After a short silence she said, 'You know your father's dead?'

He nodded.

'Mmm,' she responded. 'So, why have you come now?'

'Because it was possible… Because time has passed… Because I needed to. I've been living abroad,' he added.

'I thought so,' she replied. 'Your brother thought so too. He always said you'd come back. "Like the prodigal," he said.'

'He would,' the man replied.

'Do you want to make some tea?' she asked. 'There's cake in the tin on the table. I like having cake in the morning. You'll probably find you know where everything is.'

'How do you manage?'

'Mrs Wilson, Lottie, next door, is very helpful. She does some shopping for me. She'll put lunch out as well when she's here. She's been here a few years… since your time.'

'What happened to the Webbs?'

'I don't know. They left. The mother died of cancer I think.'

'If there's anything I can do while I'm here…'

She laughed. Then she said, 'You could paint the gate, I suppose. I don't think Mr Wilson will do it.'

He nodded and went into the kitchen to make the tea. Time had stood still in there. There was a tang of oven grease, as if layers of meals cooked over many years had been absorbed into the fabric of the kitchen and couldn't be erased by simple cleaning. The teapot was the same, the silver pot that had replaced the china one he broke as a child. He remembered to warm the pot, and to make a tray that was evenly laid out with a milk jug, sugar, teaspoons, side plates, and cups and saucers carefully taken down from the dresser.

'I see you've used the best china,' she said. 'You always did like the best. That suit looks expensive.'

'Do you want some cake?' he asked.

'Oh yes,' she said. 'I need a little treat.'

He passed her the tin and a plate. She was clearly restricted in her movement and in some pain.

'Are you not having some? There's lemon sponge…'

'I don't like cake.'

'Really?' she said. And then, 'Are you going to tell me where you live?'

'Zurich,' he said. 'I work in finance. I'm not married or anything.'

'Your brother is. But there are no children.'

They were silent for a few moments.

'Has the town changed much?' he asked.

'The place, you mean? Or the people?'

'Both.'

'I doubt there's anybody who would remember you, if that's what you mean. Lots of business people come here now. It's convenient, apparently.'

'I see they shut up the mill –'

'There's lots of different shops,' she interrupted. 'And a new library. Or was that there before?'

'It was planned,' he said.

'How long ago is it?'

'Twenty-five years.'

'A lot has happened,' she said. 'How long will you stay?'

'A week,' he replied. 'I'll be at the Bluebell. I think that's better. But I'll come and see you each day.'

'If you want to. I usually have a sleep in the afternoons.'

'Perhaps I can hire a car and take you out one day. We could go on an excursion… We could go and see the Old Windmills.'

'The what?'

'The Old Windmills. Don't you remember?'

'If you want to. Expensive mind, hiring a car.'

'That's not an issue.'

'I see,' she said.

He heard the sound of the gate swing open, recognising it without looking up. There was a cry of 'Yoohoo!' from the garden.

'It's Lottie,' she said. The back door opened.

'Oh, I'm sorry, I didn't know you had visitors.'

'It's alright. Come in. This is my other son, the one you haven't met. He lives abroad.'

'Hello. This is unexpected. Are you just visiting?'

'I'm in the country for just a few days, unpredicted,' he replied.

'That's nice,' she said. 'Shall I go ahead and put you out some lunch, or are you…?'

'Yes please,' his mother replied. 'You don't mind watching me, do you?' she said to him. 'Unless you want a meal as well?'

'I can always have cake, I'll get something later.'

They sat drinking tea in silence whilst Mrs Wilson busied herself in the kitchen.

'Have things changed much since you were last here?' she asked when she came back into the room.

'A little… Do people not use the pond in the summer anymore?'

'The pond? Oh, you mean the one down by the old mill. I don't think so. I never heard of that being used. It's shut off I think. Are you OK to get lunch out of the microwave and serve your mother when it's ready? It seems silly for me to wait, and get in your way. And my husband wants his.'

'Is he at home?' asked his mother.

'Yes… at the moment.'

'I've not heard him.'

'Good,' said Mrs Wilson, blushing. 'See you later. Good to meet you. I expect I'll see you again.'

Lunch was painfully slow. Afterwards she indicated she wanted to sleep, in her chair. 'Do you mind if I stay while you sleep?' he asked.

'What will you do?' she said.

'I'll have a walk round the garden… round the house.'

'That's alright. Go wherever you want.'

He watched her fall asleep in the chair.

The room that he had once slept in was now without personality, and had clearly been used for occasional visitors. The door to his mother's room was ajar, but he had no intention of going in there.

The middle bedroom was like a storeroom. The things that might have been put in an attic had accumulated there. He recognised the shabby green suitcase, a relic from his grandparents, with the initials E.H.H., the material flaking off like the paint on the outside gate. He put the case on a chair and clicked it open. Inside were the dregs of his childhood, preserved like a time capsule.

The choices of what had been important to keep then were revealed to the scrutiny of time: the shells and stones were meaningless, intended memories of holidays and walks, the detail long forgotten; there was a class photograph taken at his junior school, with most of the names now erased from his memory. He'd forgotten his fascination with history and the history book he'd made himself as a child, complete with his own short writings reflecting on the stories and subjects that had captured his imagination. There were school reports, copies of comics, and a few postcards. He turned the postcards over to read the messages.

The image on the colour postcard from Ilfracombe suggested a different era of English seaside holidays, but the message still resonated with him:

The weather is glorious. I'm on the beach and in the sea all day. I've got a gorgeous tan – blood-red, all over. Love from Gemma.

He shut the green suitcase and his eyes roved over the piles of boxes, bags and papers. He remembered the metal tin trunk and dragged it from under a pyramid of rolled rugs and bedding.

The stamp collection that he'd carefully assembled seemed to be intact. A significant part of the collection was the album he'd inherited from his grandfather, the album that he'd coveted as a child and that he knew was of considerable value. 'Don't you ever give that away,' was the half-fearful instruction he'd received. He felt guilty for its neglect.

Underneath the albums, some tins of stamps, and the packages of first day covers, were large, plain white envelopes, nestling at the bottom of the trunk. He didn't remember these. Inside there were wads of £50 and £20 notes. It was a considerable sum. It was a nest egg, and it was an accident waiting to happen.

He carefully replaced the collection and tin trunk as he had found them.

Later, he was sitting back downstairs with his mother, who was now awake and seemingly a little more communicative.

'So, you're doing well for yourself,' she said, slightly grudgingly, as if to confirm that life was generally unfair. 'I suppose you travel a lot?'

'Not often to this country,' he replied, half-truthfully.

'Your brother comes once a month, regularly, for the weekend. Sometimes his wife, Julia, comes with him. They seem happy.' She looked at him searchingly. 'Somehow you don't look as I would have expected,' she said. 'I don't know what it is. But your face has changed.'

'When did you get MS?' he asked.

'The diagnosis was just before your father died. But I think it was coming on a long time before that.'

'I'm sorry about that.'

'Yes… They say it can be caused by stress.'

'I see.'

'It will probably deteriorate,' she added. 'But I don't know how long it will take. I shall stay here as long as I can. Mrs Wilson is very good. I can knock on the wall if I need anything. I help her out a little. Her husband is in and out of work.'

'She's just come through the gate,' he said, past memories of insensitivities bringing a familiar wave of embarrassment.

'Well, I'm not saying anything that isn't true.'

Lottie knocked at the back door.

'Hi,' he said.

'Hello. I wondered if your mother wanted anything from the shops. I'm just on my way. Have you had a sleep?'

'I dropped off for a few moments.'

He laughed. 'It was a good couple of hours. There was time for me to find my old stamp collection.'

'My husband collects stamps,' said Mrs Wilson.

'I could never understand the fascination with them,' his mother said. 'Still, yours were quite valuable.'

'No, it was grandfather's that were of value, not mine.'

'Those are there too though, aren't they?' his mother said, sharply.

'They should probably be stored somewhere more suitable,' he said. 'It would be a pity if they deteriorated.'

Mrs Wilson jumped in, 'It's amazing the things you keep. So much of its rubbish and then there's little gems you don't want to part with. Still, what about the shops?'

'Thank you Lottie. I have a real fancy for some fish. I don't mind what sort.'

'They serve baked pike at the Bluebell,' he said.

'Are you staying there?' asked Mrs Wilson.

'Yes,' he said, annoyed that he'd revealed the information.

'Give Lottie some money, will you,' said his mother. 'I've not enough in my purse but there's some in the butter dish on the mantelpiece.'

He lifted the lid of the cracked, willow-pattern butter dish that had been pride of place for as long as he could remember. Inside was a roll of banknotes. He thoughtfully extracted a £20 note and replaced the lid.

After Mrs Wilson had left he stayed for a while longer. Conversation was fragmented and he felt that his mother was fatigued from the shock of his visit, from his unexpected return after such a long time. He gently suggested he should go, and that perhaps he might come back the next day. She acquiesced. As he left, looking at her face he had the sense that she did not believe she would see him again.

Back at the Bluebell he fell asleep on the bed and awoke, disorientated, later in the evening. In the bar Joanne was alone, and through the glass in the door he could see she looked subdued, but as he entered she greeted him by switching on an intimate smile and by providing a glass of red wine "on the house".

'So, how was mother?' she said.

'I'm not sure where to start.' He frowned.

'Sorry,' she said. 'I wasn't meaning to pry.'

Instead they talked about acting, Joanne's career and the parts she'd played. They talked about the historic cinema in the town, its recent restoration. He was a good listener.

'I like to change my appearance,' she said. 'Some actors look the same in each part, but bring something of their own to the character. I have to look as different as possible, change my face and feel completely different.'

'I know what you mean,' he said. She looked puzzled. 'But, you're finding it hard to get work at the moment?'

'Yes. It's not just the age thing.' A tension clouded the warmth and openness of her smile. 'I have to resolve a conflict between home circumstances and my career,' she said. Then after a pause, 'Basically I'm in the wrong relationship.'

They were silent for a few moments.

'Now let's come back to you,' she said. 'What really brings you back here?'

He thought for a moment. 'My mother has got MS,' he said.

'She's weak and vulnerable and keeps large sums of cash hidden around the house.'

'Wow. What do you plan to do?'

'I don't know,' he said. Then, changing the subject again, he added, 'If you're free tomorrow afternoon, would you like to come with me to the cinema? I don't want to go alone... I'd like to see it.'

She thought for a moment. 'That would be lovely.' He was surprised, but pleased.

After he left the bar he went outside, leaving Joanne to cash up with the landlord, who appeared, as if by magic, to lock up at the stroke of eleven. He was drawn by the still, cloudless sky and the comforting tingle of his arranged "date". Despite himself he found that he was walking towards the old mill.

The sound of running water and the glinting moonlight made it more attractive by night and brought a closer recollection of the place that he remembered. He took a risk and climbed the fencing onto the dam, then stood in the moonlight, absorbed in the past. He remembered that on a good day you might see a kingfisher.

Afterwards he took a long way round back to the Bluebell, anxious not to find himself alone in his room too soon. He walked down the right-of-way that had been his route to primary school and, coming out at the other end, saw Joanne walking along the opposite side of the road. He stopped, but didn't call her. As she started round the bend in the road she turned into a driveway to her left and disappeared.

He hesitated and then followed, stopping within sight of the house she'd entered, but keeping to the shadows. He noticed there was no vehicle in the drive. The house was dark, but there was a light on upstairs though the curtains were drawn shut. On the wall, by the side of the open porch, there was a plaque with the house name, visible in the moonlight – "Chandler-Wood". The name leapt out at him. It seemed to blur and then re-focus, as if his eyes were playing visual tricks. Like the credit sequences on a film the name rolled forwards, only for him to replay it. Then the light clicked off in the upstairs window and he abruptly turned and walked away.

Day Three

When she had finished her shift the night before Joanne had said to him, 'My husband may come and meet me.' As he got into bed he wondered why she had said that.

He dreamt of Mr Liddecomb and the bicycle shop.

Then he was dreaming he was inside Chandler-Wood and quietly walking up unfamiliar stairs. He opened the bedroom door. Joanne was lying in bed, alone, propped against pillows and reading with the light of a table lamp. She looked over to him and smiled, unsurprised. She put down her book and he walked over to her. As he approached she lifted her white nightdress over her head and welcomed him.

She came on top of him, uninhibited with her noise, and he felt drowned in intimacy and a new self-knowledge. It felt like completion. Finally, it felt like completion.

He woke with a feeling of pleasure, and it took a few moments to accept the disappointment when he realised he had been dreaming.

There were others in the breakfast area and Joanne was busy. As he left the room he mouthed to her that he would see her later.

His mother was expecting him and opened the door before he could ring the bell.

'There's something I want you to hear,' she said.

This time they sat in the front room, and he had the sense that a different status was being conferred. He was a visitor. There was a formality that she had not been able to impose on his first visit. On that occasion there had not been time for her to plan how to react. But now she'd been thinking about how to play this.

'Listen,' she said. She had a cassette recorder in an old music system and used her stick to press the "play" button.

The recording was a radio programme, or rather the last few minutes of a radio programme. He was puzzled. His mother stared intently into the distance. There was silence. Then the announcer's voice broke in:

And now before the weather forecast this is an urgent message for Mr Thomas Hudson, last seen fifteen years ago in the Hoddesdon area of Hertfordshire. Will Mr Thomas Hudson please get in touch urgently with his mother or with the Princess Alexandra Hospital in Harrow, as his father is dangerously ill. That is Mr Thomas Hudson, last seen in Hoddesdon in Hertfordshire fifteen years ago, please get in touch with your mother as your father is dangerously ill.

After a moment he got up and pressed the "stop" button.

'Why didn't you?' she said. 'Get in touch.'

'I didn't hear it.'

'So how did you know he was dead?'

'I was told.'

'I don't understand why you've come back. What do you want?'

'I don't want anything.'

They sat in silence.

'Look. I won't stay today,' he said. 'But I will come back again. I'm not sure why I've come after all this time. It's not an apology. Maybe it was to see what might be resolved, *whether* it could be resolved, finished, completed somehow… But I don't want to be… persecuted. Again.'

'Persecuted?' she said, wonderingly.

He got up and left the house, quietly closing the front door behind him.

The old cinema had undergone a complete facelift. At the time he was a teenager it had closed, and was not available as a venue for back-row assignations with a girlfriend. But gone now was the seedy, unpopular fleapit of his childhood. There was a different world revealed beneath the stripped interior and the careful restoration. A hidden beauty had been uncovered by the removal of the suspended ceiling to open the original vaulted roof, and the restoration of the pre-talkies foyer, previously hidden behind wooden partitions. There was also a small museum collection, available for viewing before each screening, and containing items of equipment long ago stored and forgotten in the cinema basement. There was cinema memorabilia, and stories and information about people – those connected with this particular cinema in the past, managers, staff, and customers. It revived his passion for history, something that he had put aside because of a deliberate decision to block the past. But the visit also made him think about the possibilities for personal rehabilitation.

Joanne seemed to be excited by his enthusiasm and shared her own knowledge of the cinema. They sparked together, but he sensed she was troubled when he dropped nuggets of knowledge that gave occasional glimpses of a long-held familiarity. She tentatively dropped in teasing questions -

'How long has your mother lived here?'

He responded with vague references and a smile that kept his privacy jealously guarded, noticing the attractive indecision that crossed her face when in such moments of puzzlement she wanted to ask more.

During the film they held hands. It was entirely natural. A mutually supportive gesture closed by a squeeze as they got up to leave. They had an ice cream in the foyer, but then the coldness of the ice seemed to mirror a change in the mood as their time together came to a close.

'I have to go,' she said. 'I'm not in work this evening. Thank you. It's been a lovely afternoon.'

'When… might I see you again?' he asked.

'I'll be back at the Bluebell tomorrow,' she said, closing down the question. He leant in to kiss her but she averted her face and it became an awkward hug.

After she'd gone he wandered aimlessly down the Old High Street, debating whether to go back and see his mother again. Perhaps it would be better to leave it until tomorrow, when he could once more propose the excursion to the Old Windmills. That might enable them to escape the stifling memories of the house, to a place which held more positive connections. Would that be possible?

He saw Lottie outside the flower shop, or Liddecomb's Bicycle Repairs as it had once been.

'Hey,' she said. 'Are you on your way to your mother's?'

'Not this afternoon,' he replied. Her eyes were red-rimmed and puffy. He saw she'd been crying. She looked older, though he had previously thought that she was a similar age to him.

'I get bad hay fever,' she said, noticing his attention. 'I must get something for it. Actually, I've got a prescription for your mother, do you want to…?'

'Does she need it today?' he asked quickly.

'No, it's not urgent.'

Taking it from her he said, 'I'll give it to her tomorrow. Thank you for all your help.'

'It's no trouble,' she said. 'I like going round to see her… She's been very kind to me.'

'Is she able to manage, really, living on her own? It's hard to get the true picture.'

'It's difficult,' said Lottie, 'but she puts on a brave face. She can always knock if she needs something. If I'm not there my husband probably would be. It must be hard for you, being away, abroad. Do you know, I realised after we'd met that I'd never seen your picture before. I didn't know what you looked like. I feel as if I know your brother quite well.'

He deflected the implicit questions and on the spur of the moment said, 'I'm worried about the cash she keeps around the house.' He explained with reference to the butter dish, and implied other, similar caches.

'She does lose things,' Lottie replied, sadly. She looked vulnerable and he felt suddenly as if he wanted to buy her some flowers.

As he walked down to the old mill once again, and headed for the pond, it seemed as if a different weather system set in. The sun disappeared and a grey drizzle settled that was more appropriate for October than for May. He knew he should get back to the dull comfort of the Bluebell, but with no Joanne there was nothing there but time to kill. He didn't linger at the pool but turned, and as he did so, acknowledged a man hooded in a thick waterproof, getting no response in return. Presumably walking a dog, the man was using a thick stick to search the vegetation at the side of the path as he passed.

When he got back to the mill itself he realised that he'd dropped his mother's prescription. He retraced his steps, searching the path as he went.

'Is this what you're looking for?' The stranger was standing in front of him, intimidating in tone, with the hood compressing his features that were dripping with rain. He held onto the package as if he did not intend to return it.

'Thank you.'

The stranger beat the long grass at the side of the path. 'There used to be a plaque here somewhere. Don't know where it's gone. Still, this place isn't public anymore. Did you know that?'

'Thank you,' he said again and took the package from the man's hand. He turned to leave.

The stranger spoke again. 'Mind who you get involved with. I know who you are.'

The man walked away without responding. Instinctively he thought the stranger was Joanne's husband… and he also felt he'd seen the face before.

Day Four

Joanne didn't appear at breakfast. It was served by the host, alternately jovial and put upon. 'She's not very well today,' he said.

After breakfast he steeled himself to his plan.

Passing the old library he paused to watch contractors who were erecting temporary hoarding around the site, hoardings that were covered with ominous warnings to children including prominent

DANGER signs. The purposeful flurry of activity seemed to take no account of the years of neglect.

He rang the doorbell of his mother's house and this time thought he could hear the ringing inside. But there was no answer. Nor was there any answer when he knocked loudly at the front door and called out. He wondered if she had decided not to see him, and had an image of her sitting in the back room, proud and bitter, determining to hold fast until the end.

He walked back up the hill and on impulse went into the flower shop. The scent was overpowering and added to the strangeness. He had been in the shop many times in the past but now the layout was unrecognisable. The interior had been gutted and completely refitted. He smiled to himself, thinking of the irony if he were to buy his mother flowers, and then ordered a delicate bouquet to be sent to Chandler-Wood, no message.

'I see you've kept the penny-farthing,' he said, but only received a blank look in response. 'On the side wall.'

'Oh, is that what it is. It would be too much hassle to take it down.'

He asked if there was anywhere nearby to hire a car. Then he retraced his steps towards his mother's house. This time he didn't have to wait long for a response. The door was opened, authoritatively, by a middle-aged man wearing a dog collar. 'Good morning,' he said.

'Is my mother in?' the man asked.

The clergyman hesitated momentarily and then stood aside to let him in.

His mother was sitting very upright at the table in the back room, one hand resting on her stick, and the other dispensing coffee from her best silver pot. On the table were plates with snacks and chocolate biscuits.

'I met Lottie in town yesterday and she gave me a prescription for you,' he said.

'Sit down,' she replied. 'Would you like some coffee?'

'I'm Tim Parker,' added the clergyman as he helped himself to cheese straws from a plate. The straws reminded the man of a game that he had played, many years before, on that same table.

'I called earlier,' he said. 'But I couldn't get an answer.'

'I should give you a key,' she said.

There was an awkward silence during which the clergyman thoughtfully stirred his coffee. 'Have you noticed they've finally started work on the old library?' he said.

'What are they going to do with it?' the man asked.

'It's to become a centre for young people,' Tim Parker replied. 'It's much needed. There's nothing for teenagers to do round here.'

'When did Liddecomb's stop being a bicycle shop?' the man asked his mother.

'When Mr Liddecomb and his sister died,' she replied. 'There was no one to take it over. It's been a number of different shops since then and nothing has worked. I think its Interflora now.'

'That was a sad story, about the Liddecombs,' the clergyman added.

'What was that?'

'My son knew Mr Liddecomb well,' his mother said quickly.

'What happened to him?'

Tim Parker hesitated, but then carried on. 'It happened not long after I arrived. It was very sad. I'm afraid they were victims of a robbery. Mr Liddecomb was attacked in his shop, the till was robbed, and the old man was beaten to the ground. His sister disturbed them and she was attacked too. Sadly, they both died in hospital, in a matter of days. It was a great tragedy, unprovoked and unnecessary violence.'

The man looked at his mother who was staring out of the window, as if concentrating on the garden and shutting out the vicious story that was being unfolded round her coffee table.

'It was all for a few pounds,' the clergyman added. 'They never caught who did it.'

'So that was the end of the bicycle shop.'

'Yes. It was left shut for months before anything could be done about it. I don't think anyone could take it over for that purpose. From what I understand no other face would have fitted. The shop was Mr Liddecomb.'

'How long ago was this?'

'It must be about ten years. As I said it was shortly after I arrived here. The sad thing is they suspected it was someone the Liddecombs knew, possibly someone local. The town took a long time to get over it. There was a strong sense of distrust, not being sure whether the faces we passed in the street were the faces we really thought they were.'

'Yes. These things do take a long time,' the man replied.

His mother turned sharply to him. 'You're just here for a week?'

'I am,' he replied. He paused. 'I wondered if you'd like to go out tomorrow for the day? For an excursion. To the Old Windmills, I thought.'

'Do we have to decide now?' she said.

'No.'

'The spare key is on the mantelpiece. You'd better take it while we remember.'

'The Old Windmills? What are they?' Tim Parker asked. 'Could I take another cheese straw?'

It rained for much of the rest of the day and after he left his mother the man was confined to the Bluebell. He drank far too much red wine, sitting on his own in the bar, and exchanging occasional bursts of conversation with the landlord. Joanne was apparently laid up with "women's problems".

He carefully raised the subject of the Liddecombs and found that the prevailing view was that they had been victims of some passing thugs, who had taken advantage of the frailty of the shop-keeper to take a few pounds' easy pickings. They hadn't expected any resistance from the old man, and the chance robbery had gone horribly wrong.

'It wouldn't have been anyone local,' the landlord said. 'We'd have known who did it.'

Later, in early night-time dreams, the man found himself alternating between the locations of the mill pond and his mother's house. He was convinced he had to find the plaque that Joanne's husband had told him about and was hunting desperately through the undergrowth, continuously frustrated in his search, which became increasingly frantic. Even when he woke up in the night he was still half convinced that he had to continue looking, and felt as if he should get dressed immediately in order not to waste time.

Then, falling asleep again, his exchanges with his mother became bitter. She finally informed him that she only had one son, his brother, to whom she would be leaving all her property. 'You're dead to me,' she said. 'You have been for a long time.' He sat bolt upright in bed for a moment. Then he lay back and entered a deep, dreamless sleep.

Day Five

He knew he'd had far too much to drink the night before when he was woken by a knock at the door and realised he'd missed breakfast.

It was the landlord.

'You have a visitor,' he said. 'Can you come down?'

The feeling of nausea slowed his getting dressed, and was reinforced by a sense of foreboding. The landlord's voice had not been encouraging. He had sounded quiet, almost dismayed, lacking the bonhomie that was usually part of his make-up. The man anticipated that he was going to find Joanne's husband in the Bluebell reception, the situation made more uncomfortable by her working relationship with the place. Instead, he found two police officers sitting in the bar. They stood up when he came in.

'Mr Hudson?'

He paused. 'That's me.'

They invited him to sit.

'You don't look too well.'

He was silent, wanting them to come to the point. When they did the dizziness was overwhelming and he only just made it into the toilets. Through his sickness he was aware that one of the policemen had followed him. He held onto the basin. The ground seemed to be collapsing beneath him. Despite everything the worst feeling was the uncontrollable retching.

His legs were shaking so that his knees knocked against the pedestal. Sweat was running down his face. Eventually he ran cold water onto his hands and wiped his mouth and forehead. He looked at himself in the mirror. The image was finally still and looking at his reflection no longer brought back the nausea.

His face, though, seemed to have changed overnight. He could see what he might be like in late middle age. In the corner of the glass reflection he could also see the policeman staring at him, leaning against the cubicle door. The policeman looked curious.

'Feeling better?'

He looked directly at the policeman through the mirror and was subjected to another wave of vomiting. It was strained and unrewarding, producing a tiny stream of bilious yellow liquid. The taste in his mouth was excruciating. He drank some water. He held his grip on the basin for some time. It was a way of holding on to reality.

'When did you find her?' he asked, finally.

'It was the neighbour,' he replied. 'She called the vicar first for some reason. The vicar called us.'

They went back through to the bar. The other policeman was drinking coffee and talking avidly to the landlord. He stopped abruptly when they re-entered.

'When you're ready we need to ask you some questions. It's probably better we don't do that here.'

The landlord looked stonily at the man and left the room.

Getting into the police car he found himself conjuring up images of his cinema trip with Joanne. He vaguely wondered why they were just still images, like snapshots. Then he thought he might be sick again in the car, but they drove carefully, slowly. His legs were weak when he came to get out, and he thought he knew what it must be like to be old, to have MS like his mother.

Gathering the story was like piecing together a jigsaw. He was not given all the facts as a single narrative. It was as if they were testing his response.

'Do you want me to see her?' he said.

'Not just yet,' was the response.

The disorientation that was partly the result of his hangover contributed to the lack of clarity. It was as if the discussion skirted the important facts and focused on the banality of details of his visits to his mother. Whilst he felt embarrassed by the evening spent consuming carafes of red wine at the Bluebell, it really seemed immaterial in relation to the fact that his mother was dead.

After a while the policemen seemed content to sit quietly and to let him absorb the information they had proffered.

His mother was dead. She had been found by Lottie Wilson, who for some reason had called Tim Parker as well as an ambulance. 'She knew there was nothing that could be done,' they said. It was only later that the man understood that Lottie knew that nothing could be done because his mother had been savagely beaten about the head. Lottie had found her on the floor, in her bedroom where she had been attacked.

He started to understand the circuitous way that he was being asked questions and also started to see information provided by Tim Parker behind some of these. The clergyman clearly knew a good deal about the relationship between him and his mother; she had talked to him at length. He half thought the door might open for the policemen to respectfully make way for their superior officer, Mr Parker.

He didn't know what they expected of him. They seemed courteous, kindly even, but there was no framework to the questioning, no indication of how long they intended to ask him to stay, or how things might progress.

After a while they left him, temporarily, with coffee and toast, and he found himself thinking, not of his mother and the appalling events that had unfolded, but of Joanne. Of whether she knew what had happened, whether she was even now back in work at the Bluebell, and of her husband who had accosted him down by the mill. There was something about that he hadn't yet understood.

When they came back, they asked him about any items of value in his mother's house. He told them about the cash, of at least two places where it was deposited, and of his concerns. Then, realising this was also about a robbery, he mentioned the stamps.

They were interested. Was the collection of any real value? What did it contain? They also asked him why he had stayed at the Bluebell under an assumed name. After that they left him alone again, for a while.

In the early afternoon they took him back to the house. The busy activity around the old library building had ceased, there had been an assumed license to down tools. As if waiting for a royal procession the gardens and doorways of the street were lined with people. He was led into the place that had once been his home as if he was the one with multiple sclerosis, needing help with every step. It was clear he was to look but not touch.

The contents of the green suitcase had been strewn around the house. His childhood and life there, which only the day before had been hidden, obliterated even, were displayed in every room for all to see. The tin trunk had also been rifled. Pages had been torn from the stamp album and abandoned, individual stamps lay fluttering on the floor, the soul of the collection vandalised in a way that stabbed his heart. He wanted to protect what was left, to ease the burden of his guilt.

They led him upstairs and into the only room he had not entered on his previous visits, his mother's bedroom. They did not warn him as to what he might see. But there was no body. That had been taken, though its position was marked on the floor. He stared at the outline that had been his mother's shape, the unmade bed, the drawers pulled out, and the ransacked room. The only space left untouched was the dressing table, a shrine of photographs: his father at various times in his life, some relatively recent and showing a leaner, gaunt figure with sad eyes. His brother, and presumably wife, featured, along with older Edwardian and Victorian photographs, black and white and sepia, of various long-dead relatives, unnamed and now, probably, to remain so. And in the middle of the display was a photograph of him as a teenager, standing smiling by the Old Windmills, the day of the excursion that he remembered so well, the excursion that he had planned to repeat. It was one of the last moments of a more carefree, normal childhood. He went to pick up the photograph, but they stopped him.

He wanted to be alone, in that room, with the photograph. It was the first time for twenty-five years that he'd seen his face before the age of eighteen.

Downstairs in the back room, they asked him about the key he had been given. Had he used it, tried it even? Was it for the back door? Did he still have it? Had he used the back way through the entry at all? They showed him a small metal object and asked if he recognised it. It was the toffee hammer that had always been kept on the sideboard – decorative, as far as he knew – he never remembered it being used to crack toffee. It was small and delicate, though he could recall weighing the head in his hand and wondering what made it so heavy.

Tentatively, he asked whether his mother had knocked on the wall, tried to attract Lottie's help. He remembered her words: *she can always knock if she needs something*. The policemen didn't seem to understand. They were puzzled by his comment. They wanted him to go outside though, through the white, peeling gate he had once painted, across the Wilsons' back garden and back down the alleyway to the street. It seemed shorter, smaller than he remembered. There were many more items, including stamps, discarded in the entry itself, though he thought that these were from his own collection rather than his grandfather's album.

Back on the street a crowd had gathered outside his mother's front door. It was good they had returned via the entry and he could be bundled quickly into the waiting car. As he got into the car the crowd became aware of his presence and turned. He heard the shout of 'murderer!' and caught a glimpse of Joanne's accusing husband.

Returning to the police station they surprised him by asking about the Old Windmills. They wanted to know about the planned excursion with his mother, and what the windmills meant. What was their significance? Why had his mother kept that particular picture of him, at that place? He realised his mother had talked of the day to the clergyman, perhaps to others. It had clearly been of importance to her. Then they asked again why he had booked into the Bluebell under an assumed name. He showed them his passport.

It was much later in the day that, finally, they asked him about Gemma.

'After all, that's why you left here, wasn't it? That's why you've not been back, until now?'

He could feel that his left leg was jerking from the knee, his heel catching the ground, making a rhythmic rasping against the concrete floor. They watched him silently, focusing on the movement of his leg. He was reminded of when he used to sit on the edge of the dam at the mill, his legs hanging over, drumming his heel against the concrete wall.

He had never before described what had happened, told the whole story fully. It had always become corrupted by questioning, by insinuation, by the judgement of others, or simply because he didn't have the words, or the resilience, to tell it simply, truthfully as it was. Perhaps he had never been able to confront the reality, not just of the events that had happened, but also of their meaning for him.

Eventually he said, 'Gemma and I knew each other for a while. I'd always liked her a lot. Then, the summer it happened, we got together properly at a party. It all became very intense, from my side. Her parents were not happy. They thought I was too serious. I think they thought I was dangerous.'

His leg stopped moving and there was complete silence in the room. He was aware they were looking at him directly, expectantly, and he recognised the hardening of feeling against him.

'I was older than her, of course. She probably saw it as something fun, no more. If I had thought that at the time it would have been devastating.'

One of the officers spoke. 'She was a kid really, wasn't she?'

He ignored the interruption. 'I worshipped her.'

'We started going out together. I got very jealous when she went places without me, when she had other friends. She could sometimes be a tease. But she liked the way I liked her. We didn't do anything, of course.'

'Her parents monitored you?'

'There was no need,' he replied. 'She was only fourteen, nearly fifteen… I was responsible.'

'Responsible?'

'Yes. I had plans for the future, going to university, having her come to stay. Making sure we could remain together. Bringing her parents round. I wanted to chase that worried look off her father's face… The mill pond was a magnet, then. It had a different face to the one you see now.' He paused. 'Have you worked here, lived here long?' he asked them.

His leg was jerking back and forth again. They were watching his foot whilst listening intently, it seemed, for the sound of his shoe contacting the floor. Neither of them replied.

'The mill was operating during the week, the paths were open and the pond was accessible... It was somewhere to go in the summer. People had picnics in the meadow at weekends, families went there. I can't believe how different it looks now. The water always seemed clear, the force of it through the sluice kept it constantly moving. It was clear and pure. The day it happened we bunked off school. I persuaded her to bunk off school.'

'We went to the mill. I'd got bottles of cider. It was a sunny day, at least at first, bright and clear. There was no one else there. It felt very intimate. Well, why should there be anyone else there? It was a working day, not a holiday. That's why we bunked off. That's why I took her there. We expected to be alone.

The cider made us relaxed, adventurous. I was very intense as always and she was OK with that, responded to it. Or so I thought. Perhaps she was simply humouring me. I don't know. It seemed like we were the only people in the world. We were close, cuddling and kissing. I talked a lot about how much I loved her. We didn't do anything.

Then she dared me to go into the water. She dared me.

I don't know why. Perhaps she'd got bored. I probably wouldn't have done it if I hadn't had a drink. I'm not a good swimmer. I don't like swimming. Not even on holidays. I don't like the cold. And the mill was cold. I learnt late, in school, when we had to go to swimming lessons. Technically I could swim, but that was all. She dared me to go into the water. I would have done anything for her approval. So I went in.

I went in... without any clothes. It was very cold. I only stayed in a minute or two. Then I stood shivering on the bank and she laughed. The sun had gone in and I couldn't get warm. Then I said it was her turn and that after that we'd warm each other. It was a mutual commitment somehow.

I can see the look in her eyes. She seemed high, on cider and adventure, and on our promise. It was a wicked look. She took off her skirt and blouse. She had short, dark hair, a single wave running through it. Sometimes she swept it behind her ear. She never took her eyes off me. It was as if our eyes were glued together. That look she gave me, before she went in. It seemed like the moment beyond which we would become something else again, complete. I've never felt again such a sense of expectation.

Then she smiled and plunged in. Not a cautious wading, gauging the depth and the cold, as I had done. She did it without fear, for the moment. She swam straight out to the middle, treading the current. It must have been the drink. That was my fault. That was my responsibility.

I suppose she was a hundred feet away, treading water, and she waved, that same look on her face. Then she went under the water and I watched to see where she'd reappear. But she didn't. She didn't come back up. Of course, I realised something was wrong.'

He felt as if his whole body was jerking now, not just his leg, but those watching and listening were still intently observing his foot, as if that was the fulcrum of events.

'I didn't know what to do. Why should I have known what to do? I had a car accident once, years later, and moments after it was over and the collision had occurred, I pressed the horn. I kept my palm on it. There's no logic. It's something you do. It was like that. I was responsible for a fourteen-year-old girl drowning and all I could do was to call her name as if she was going to pop back up out of the water.'

'Did you not go in… try and find her?'

'I told you. It was a cloudless day at first. When I came out of the water, the first time, the sun had gone in. I couldn't get warm. I was shaking with cold. I did wade back in. It was too late. The water was dark. It didn't seem clear any more. Then there was a shout from the dam. "What are you doing?" they said. I suppose I was standing there, naked in the water. I dived in then. I couldn't see anything. I couldn't see her.

It was death by misadventure. But of course it was my fault. I took her out of school, I gave her drink, and I encouraged her to go in. I didn't rape her. I didn't take advantage of her. I didn't drown her deliberately. I didn't run away. I didn't abdicate responsibility. I did none of those things, though of course they were all said.'

His leg still moved.

'I can understand the attacks. I can understand the feelings of her family. But I never understood my mother's response. I never understood her persecution. She couldn't accept the circumstances, didn't trust my intentions, she wouldn't believe my feelings. I wanted to see if I could make any sense of that now, after all this time. That's why I came back.'

After he'd finished there was a silence for a while. Then one of the policemen spoke.

'Did you know she still has family here?'

'No… I think I assumed they would have long gone. It was a long time ago. Twenty-five years. In any case I wasn't expecting to be recognised. I changed my name. Not just for now. I have a different name, as you know. And my face has changed. I'm not eighteen anymore.'

'There's still a lot of people here who remember the incident. There is strong local feeling. There always is with these things. The story is still told. You are still talked about. Now it has been revived. You're not forgiven.'

'I wouldn't expect to be,' he said. 'What matters is whether I forgive myself.'

'Word has got around, following the attack on your mother. Feelings are running very high.'

The second policeman spoke for the first time, quietly but with authority. 'We think you're going to be better off staying here rather than going back to the Bluebell.'

The man nodded.

Later, he could not get any relief from the pain in his left ankle. Something had happened whilst telling his story, jerking his leg, and the constant aching prevented him from finding any comfort, even in sleep. Nor would they provide him with any painkillers.

It drove him back again to the past, to the memory of slipping and falling on the stairs at home, twisting his left ankle. He had carried too much on the tray upstairs, loading it in order to make a point, ensuring that all was there, correct and in order. Afterwards he had been confined, walking for a while with a stick. That was when they had gone on the excursion to the Old Windmills, just him and his mother. That was the last time everything had been normal. It was also the first time he had really become aware of Gemma.

The Old Windmills was actually a single windmill, in private ownership. It was a house with a small attached business, and though it had been lovingly restored and the sails maintained, it didn't operate as a windmill anymore. What made the place a real attraction was the series of large-scale installations, created by the owner and open to the public. Each was a simple figure – a flapping scarecrow, a mother bathing a child, a man fishing – installations that sprang to life through an accompanying, wind-operated mechanism, each like a small windmill.

Apparently, the concept had been created when the owner had started his wrought iron company. They were a means to promote the business, but had become a quirky attraction in their own right, particularly appealing to families. It was from this place that the gate at home had been purchased. A promise had been made by his mother that on some occasion they would go to the Old Windmills and see the installations, and the place where the attractive gateway had come from. When he twisted his ankle that provided two opportunities – the time for him to paint the iron work, and a spur to the visit, even though by now he was a little old to really appreciate the magic.

It was a Saturday. It was his special treat. His father was working and his younger brother was left with friends. He was still walking with a stick, quite proud of the attention it attracted, and was excited by the trip, but it was the young girl he met there that dominated his attention. She was with her family, a young sister, mother and father, and she was intrigued by his stick, his injury. They struck up a friendship, exploring the installations, playing mock games around them, hiding from the precocious and interfering kid sister. He felt a little guilty when he saw his mother sitting at a table, with the remains of their picnic, watching them with a strange look on her face. On the way home she had said she thought he was growing up. Shortly after that he stopped needing the stick.

He would see Gemma around and they always acknowledged each other. There was a connection, a bond, waiting for the right moment. The party was the right moment.

Finally, the pain in his ankle eased and he fell into a fitful sleep. In his dream the police questioning became more aggressive and he acknowledged they suspected him of attacking his mother himself. They seemed to think he had beaten her with a stick and stolen the stamp collection. He pointed out that the stamp collection belonged to him anyway. Lottie could verify that, as she'd been there when they talked about it. Then he was walking back down his mother's street at night, the first evening he'd arrived, before anything had happened, and he saw again the neighbour in the window, Mr Wilson's face pressed against a small pane of glass, briefly watching him. It was an antagonistic stare. He woke up and knew instantly why he'd recognised the man at the mill pond and the face shouting 'murderer' in the crowd. It wasn't Joanne's husband after all, it was Lottie's, the enigmatic man next door who was also into stamps.

Day Six

In the morning his ankle had stopped hurting and he had that sense of lucidity that can sometimes come through sleep. It was a new clarity about why he had returned at this time, what he had hoped to seek in the way of absolution and completion. Instead, he had been present when someone had smashed his mother's skull with a toffee hammer.

He didn't know what to expect when the policemen came into the interview room. Perhaps they would seriously consider him a suspect. Or maybe he'd be subjected to yet a further round of questioning about his role in the events of a long distant past. Could they change a verdict all these years later, satisfy media and public appetite for scapegoats by digging up a previous tragedy? He hadn't considered the possibility of Gemma's parents still living there. How would they be feeling about this and about him?

Instead, they showed him a picture and asked if he knew the person. It was an unattractive male face, and a man he recognized. Then they wanted to know more about where his mother hid cash and about the likely value of his grandfather's stamps. They produced the battered and dismembered album and asked if he could indicate anything of particular value that had been taken. As far as he could see the stamp album pages had been torn out randomly, though certainly some of the more interesting examples had gone. But how many of these were lying discarded around the house? Then they asked about his contact with Lottie, and particularly about how much he'd talked with her about his mother, her circumstances and her future plans.

Then, he asked them about the family, Gemma's family. 'You said they were still here.'

They were surprised that he was more interested in that than in progress on finding his mother's killer.

'I know the family,' said one of the policemen. 'One of the parents is dead and the other is in a local nursing home.'

'Which one is still alive?' he asked.

'Mr Chandler is in the home, he has a degenerative illness – Alzheimer's, I think. However, there was a sister. She still lives in the town. You've met her... she works at the Bluebell. She was a child when it happened.'

Later, he wondered on what basis he was still staying at the police station, but was disinclined to ask. Mainly he wondered when Joanne would have been told, or learnt, who he was. Or did she already know? He tried to capture a picture of her as an eight-year-old, playing at the Old Windmills, but could only bring back vague recollections. His image of Gemma was crystal clear.

He was left alone for most of the day and the revelation, when it came, was towards the end of the evening. An arrest had been made. Michael Wilson had been charged with breaking and entering, with robbery and with the murder of his mother. There was no implication that Lottie had been involved in any of the events of that night. However, his mother's failure to knock for help probably indicated her confusion, in that the attack had come from the person next door.

Informally they advised him that they'd been called to the Wilsons' house once over an issue of domestic violence. More importantly, Michael had a history as a young man and had been considered a potential suspect in the Liddecomb assault. The view seemed to be that that attack might also now be finally resolved.

Day Seven

In the morning he left the police station and made one further visit to his mother's house. His meeting with his brother was cordial but short. They had little to say to each other, and it was clear that his brother had long since closed the chapter of his family life relating to his sibling.

Back at the Bluebell he packed his limited belongings, including the photograph of the Old Windmills that he had taken from the house. Before he left the room he opened the envelope he'd found on the dressing table, addressed "to David". It was a note from Joanne.

Dear David

That's how I know you, so I shan't call you Tom.

I'm so sorry about what has happened to your mother. There are no words…

I also wanted to let you know that now I know who you are, it doesn't make any difference to how I feel about the time we spent together. It was good.

I was very young when it happened. I remember a family trip to the Old Windmills, and Gemma teasing Tom and taking his stick. I can't picture Tom, though I must have seen you after that. I remember my father's anger, even before it happened. Most of all I remember the sense, afterwards, of wishing everything would go back to being normal. I guess it never did, for Tom.

I hope things do go back to being normal for you. Take good care.

Joanne

When David finally went downstairs, the landlord was pleasant, but subdued, affirming he was glad the room would be free as he'd already got a provisional booking for the next day. As David paid his bill they even had a little joke about his name change.

Coming out of the Bluebell, David paused momentarily and then purposefully took a left turn, away from the station and back down towards the mill. The weather was glorious.

As he walked along the path towards the pond he thought

about the eight-year-old Joanne. He tried to remember her face, to chart the physical transition to the woman she had become. And suddenly she was there in front of him. She was crouched in the grass at the side of the path, wearing gloves, clearing the weeds. He stopped and she looked up.

'I thought you might come back,' she said. 'There's a little stone cross here. My father had it put there to remember Gemma. I've not been great at maintaining it. I thought it was time to clean it up.'

He knelt down beside her. 'Thank you for your note,' he said. He touched the cross.

'You loved her a lot, I think.'

'So, you remember the trip to the Old Windmills?' he said.

'They're not there anymore,' she replied. 'The business stopped and the windmill was sold. The new owner let the installations go and eventually they were taken down. Pity.'

He opened his bag and took out the photograph. 'I wouldn't have recognised you,' she said. 'Your face does seem to have changed, as well as your name.'

'Everything that has happened…' he started and then stopped.

'Go on,' she said.

'Meeting you has been very important. Tell me, why is your house called Chandler-Wood?'

'How did you know that?' She paused and he did not reply. 'Well, I wanted to keep the name Chandler somewhere when I married. Maybe I was thinking about Gemma still. Wood is my husband's name. I guess it was also about connection, commitment.'

'What are you going to do?'

'Commitment is very important. You know that. I'm going to stay committed to my acting… and to my husband.'

'I hope it works for you.'

'Maybe, in another time, another world… we would have…'

'I know.' He stood up, held out his hand and she took it. He helped her up. 'I think it's time to say goodbye,' he said. He went to give her a hug but instead she kissed him, fully, on the mouth. She looked him straight in the eyes.

'Take good care,' she said.

He nodded. 'And you.' Then, without going on to the pond, he started back up the path.

David turned and waved, and momentarily felt his left ankle give way, as if the ground was dropping beneath him. Then it was normal again and he walked away without looking back.

At the shop near the station, the shop that had once belonged to Mr Liddecomb, he arranged for flowers to be sent for his mother's funeral. On the card he wrote *Sorry for everything. Goodbye. Tom.*

David did not have to wait long on the platform. The train that pulled in was modern, with a push-button door-opening device. He sat down and savoured the momentary darkness as the train pulled away through the tunnel, taking him back towards Zurich… another life.

SANCTUARY

A s Easter and the anniversary drew closer, Anna grew increasingly restless at her desk. When Richard returned each weekend he made a point of enquiring about her novel. She would reply that progress was slow and he would smile in a way that was intended to show support. In reality she knew that the smile reflected his smug certainty, and hope, that she was wasting her time.

Anna felt that each was too frightened to unpick the pattern of call and response which if questioned would shatter the convenience of their lives together. Looking out of her study window at the steeple of the familiar Cotswold village church, Anna daydreamed instead of writing. In her mind she saw the small memorial stone laid in the churchyard floor, anticipated the approach of another anniversary marking its inception, and in her imagination dreamt a past that was not directly to do with her novel.

Like a reformed addict, Anna now resisted the temptation to regularly visit the memorial. In the early days, Richard told her, she had frequented *that place* to the point of public humiliation. His reaction had been a shock. She hadn't known that he cared about local opinion, though she was fully aware he disapproved of her literary interest in the occult and premonition. More importantly, she had learnt that at least part of him despised her.

Richard disappeared during the week to a small London flat and a glamorous job in television. He wanted a rural idyll in which to spend his weekends, not the reality of a close, gossiping community. Anna had always felt that this same reality would offer her the material that she sought for her work. She had not anticipated the material that she had found.

It had become a tradition, over the twelve years that they had lived in the village, for Anna to prepare baskets of spring flowers for church on Good Friday. At the same time she created her own special tribute to be placed by the stone in the churchyard. Richard was not averse to that, even though the gesture was not appreciated by all. It was as if the village secretly resented Anna for hijacking their one claim to notoriety and making it her own. The memorial to the young couple, almost hidden in the churchyard, behind the west wall, became cruelly known as Anna's folly.

Each year the local rector hoped that in his Easter sermons he could avoid reference to the events which, now exactly thirteen years before, had briefly given the village a national profile. Secretly he bore his own burden of guilt that it should have occurred in his parish. Each year, like Anna, he became disturbed as the anniversary approached, knowing that her tributes in particular would revive the inevitable reminiscence and gossip. But he also realised that it would be expected that he should mark the occasion. After the Easter Sunday service a stream of once-a-year churchgoers would hover to revisit the events and to gaze reverently at the freshly decorated shrine. Anna's presence seemed to bring immediacy and a newly minted melancholy to the event itself.

Community resentment rooted in the fact that Anna had not lived there at the time of the incident. She and Richard had arrived almost a year later, and with enough distance from the horror to identify with the romance. It had also been whispered by some in the village that Richard might be planning to make a sensational television documentary about the events. Other villagers, however, knowingly pointed to Anna's intense interest, and connected her personally with the tragedy.

Anna's first visit to the village church, twelve years before, had led her into what she perceived as a labyrinth, and it took her a while to unravel and understand the full story. It was the weekend before Easter and the day before their second wedding anniversary. They had been in their new home for a matter of weeks. Despite their anniversary Richard would be returning to work on the Sunday night. He had sold Anna a move to the country on the basis of the opportunity it would afford her to write, not least given his absence during the week. But she had sulked when she learnt that he would be unable to extend his weekend so that they could be together. As a result he had diplomatically agreed to her wish that they attend a first Sunday morning service together at the village church.

Anna recalled noting the impressive carving of the church door knocker, but did not remember any of the faces from that initial congregation. She remembered being intensely aware of the numbers attending, far more than she had expected, of the charged atmosphere and of the strained face of the rector. The strength of an unarticulated bond made the assembly of people around her seem unreal. It was as if she and Richard had slipped into a parallel universe where everything looked similar and yet all was subtly different.

When the rector spoke he acknowledged this special service, the family and friends visiting from long distance, and the desperate sorrow of their return one year after the tragic circumstances which had changed their lives forever. He showed an anxiety which almost stopped him functioning. Anna felt transfixed with uncertainty about the event into which they had unwittingly trespassed. She felt her own horror through Richard's tension and she knew that he would be feeling humiliated by what appeared to be their invasive presence, and would blame her. They walked home silently and, in relief to be away from the church and the visiting congregation, made violent love on the bedroom floor. Twelve years ago.

At first local people had been eager to talk. Anna felt that an explanation of their intrusion at the anniversary service should have been broadcast in the parish magazine – expiation for the benefit of the whole community. But the community wanted to know about Anna and Richard as much as Anna wanted to understand the tragedy. She heard it from different angles, and supplemented first-hand accounts with newspaper reports, including profiles of the two young people. The community hardened in their belief that this curiosity fed a professional interest. There was unspoken division between those who disapproved of this interest and those who wished to confirm their leading role in any future account.

In fact Richard and Anna had been unaware of the sensational happenings in the village one year prior to their house purchase. At least unaware that this was the place where the events had taken place. The story was the death, in a fire, of a romantic young couple on a camping holiday. The couple had become familiar and not unwelcome figures in the village during their two-week stay.

Anna became obsessed, and as her own marriage deteriorated, so the unchanging relationship between the dead couple increasingly fed her imagination. She felt no sense of an occult presence or of any ongoing communication, but was magnetised by the plain Portland stone tablet set in the churchyard floor. It recorded only initials, the words *Died Easter Saturday*, the year, and then the touch of sentiment – *Too young but together*. It informed her novel.

Now, twelve years on, as Anna procrastinated on her writing and daydreamed at her desk, Easter drew near and the anniversary of the fire approached once more. It was always now marked at Easter weekend, whenever that fell. To Anna it meant the annual acknowledgment of the village tragedy and her own silent and floral tribute to that event. The hurried exchange of wedding anniversary gifts between her and Richard was no longer of consequence. On Good Friday she could legitimately revisit the memorial and renew her acquaintance with the young people she had never known, except in photograph and obituary, and who she only understood in the completeness of their death, then silence.

Good Friday came and on this visit Anna stood by the stone, looking at her flowers and wishing away her own life, before returning to the church to collect her baskets.

In the church porch, which always smelt musty and oozed damp, a stranger was gently tracing the outline of the impressive carving of the door knocker. He was humming, so quietly that only intermittent bars were audible, unaware of Anna as she watched. It was a conscious hum, but one which seemed to Anna to come from far, far away. All the time he stroked the lines of the carving. Then he looked up and flushed deeply, like a child caught in deceit, and started as if to justify himself. Anna was moved by his vulnerability.

'It's believed to date from the time of the Black Death,' she told him. 'The image represents a journey's end. Arrival at sanctuary.'

He smiled. 'I thought it was to do with witches.' He stepped out of the porch into the Easter sunlight and sighed deeply as if to release an inner tension.

Anna felt vaguely troubled by the mention of witches, but then she said, 'You were humming and looked so absorbed. I'm sorry to have disturbed you.'

'Perhaps I was. It really doesn't matter.'

'Would you like to see the church?' Anna offered. 'Or have you already been inside?'

He seemed to look at her for the first time, emerging from some secret place far away.

'Thank you,' he replied, and followed her in.

He moved around the church with the same care with which he'd examined the door knocker. He was sensitive to the atmosphere and to her mood. As she took possession of the baskets he appreciated the flowers, understanding that Anna was responsible. His reaction made her realise with a shock how little she had come to expect such courtesy.

By the time they came back outside a comfortable feeling had developed between them. Anna didn't know why she said, 'I'd like to show you the churchyard,' but he obediently followed her.

They picked their way through scores of village lives, the stranger stopping to examine dates, relationships and epigraphs with an intense concentration. She knew that she was leading him to the memorial. The focus of their journey had an inevitability of which he seemed to almost be aware.

At the stone tablet she was brim-full of expectation. She watched his attention flicker across the wording and take in the tribute. He looked away, uneasy. She wanted to explain, to share her passion for the spent lives of two people crystallised in youth, to share her own disappointment. He was looking at her curiously, understanding her pain in some way and yet almost fearful of her unspoken emotion. Words failed Anna. She crouched down and wept.

For a moment he tensed and she felt that he might leave, anxious to allow her privacy in her distress. Then he leant forwards and touched her on the arm, supportively. She realised he must think that they were her family.

'It's alright. I don't know these people,' she said.

He looked at her wonderingly.

'I'm not very happy,' she explained, 'and there's a story to this stone which is very moving.'

'Tell me,' he said.

'It's a long story.'

'I've plenty of time,' he replied.

She stood up and they walked away in silence. As they left the churchyard she spoke. 'Thirteen years ago, at Easter, a couple died in the village. That is a memorial to them. They'd been camping here and there was a terrible accident with a gas burner. Their tent caught fire.'

Anna hesitated. 'They were burnt to death.'

After a moment she went on, 'I decorate the plaque every Easter. There's no one else locally to do it as they weren't from round here. It was our village tragedy, horror story really. Two people who died very young and who apparently cared very much for each other, who would have made a success of their relationship. I couldn't bear to see the shrine left unacknowledged.'

She glanced at the stranger. He looked anxious, sensitive either to her or to her tale. They walked on.

'What about you?' he said at last. 'Why are you unhappy? What's the connection with this… tragedy that it moves you so much?'

'This is my house,' she said. 'Won't you have some coffee?'

She expected him to politely decline and to make his escape, but instead he made a sound of affirmation and they turned into the cottage gateway. As they scrunched their way up the gravel drive Anna felt as if she should walk on tiptoe. But there was nobody to hear them.

At the door she turned to him. 'I live here with my husband. He's away during the week, in the city. He works in television. I work from home.'

He flushed.

Anna opened the unlocked front door. 'We'll go into my study,' she said. 'I like the view of the church.'

He followed, silently obeying her as if he had no will of his own.

'What is it that you do?'

'I try and write,' she replied. 'Novels, or rather a novel. The truth is that I've had the occasional short story published and, five years ago, one small volume of stories. It's not a lot to show for twelve years.'

'Is that why you're unhappy?'

'Perhaps. It's a long story.'

'I've plenty of time,' he replied, once again.

Anna smiled, unsure as to whether or not he was mocking her. 'Why do you have so much time?'

'I'm staying here on holiday… On my own,' he added. There was a pause. 'Sad really, isn't it.' They both laughed and the tension was broken. Anna went to make the coffee.

In the kitchen she put together a tray, selecting continental white breakfast cups, a stone white jug of cream and coarse, demerara sugar. Hesitantly, she took a small bottle of whisky from the pantry and placed it on the base beside the Aga. She picked up the card that had arrived from Richard the day before. It was a picture post-card of the sights of London, a card he'd clearly picked up at an

Underground kiosk, flying between appointments. Even the writing was hurried: *Filming in Withernsea. Unable to get back over the weekend. Will phone you from the hotel.* Unable to get back for Bank Holiday weekend? Where was Withernsea? She was frightened of the implications that might arise if she found out. Anna had not been able to look at the card again until now. With the coffee jug prepared she decisively added the whisky bottle and two glasses, before carrying the tray through to the study.

He was standing, staring out of the window at the church, as if intent on memorising every detail. 'How long have you lived here?' he asked suddenly.

'Just over twelve years.'

'Then you didn't live here when this accident happened?'

'No... I suppose I've just adopted it.' She felt embarrassed.

'Have you been unhappy for all of that time?'

'Mostly.' She moved towards him at the window and placed the tray on her desk. He was studying the books, carefully laid out research material and background reading for her novel. She felt panicked that he would draw the wrong conclusions from the subject matter – the supernatural, local hauntings...

'Witches,' he said.

'I'm not one,' she replied.

'I know,' he said. Then time slipped as if the film had jumped and she found that she had laid her head against his shoulder and that they both had arms around each other. The tears were rolling down her face as she kissed him.

There was the same wondering look in his eyes as she'd seen in the churchyard. It was sympathetic and curious. She led him, with conviction, to the couch and once again he seemed compliant and obedient. She felt confident in his willingness to be led. He was passive as she stroked his face and kissed his head. She stepped away and unbuttoned her blouse, exposing her breasts. He looked, absorbing the picture of her body in a way that was different to the anonymous, indifferent lust that she was used to from Richard. She stepped out of her skirt and rejoined him on the couch. She so much wanted him to touch her but she sensed that he was still reluctant to take the lead. He allowed her to undress him and then she took his hand and placed it between her legs. As if disturbed from a dream he became engaged and their coupling became a partnership. As she rode him in a long-forgotten ecstasy, her pleasure was made more urgent by the realisation that she did not know his name. He was a lover, a carefree and sensitive lover, taking away the tension of her unresolved marital conflict, making her anew through this spontaneous and dangerous act of love.

After she had come, she lay blissfully still, comforted in his touch, free in the stickiness which had glued them together.

They lay together in the silent house. Finally she got up, poured the whisky and lifted the glass to his mouth. He let her trickle the warm fluid between his lips and after she had drunk they kissed and tasted the liquor on each other.

'Sanctuary,' he murmured.

'Witches,' she replied. Looking into his eyes the connection seemed complete. Whisky had dribbled from the glass and onto his body. She licked it away and their passion revived. This time he was active and made love to her with his own urgency dominant. She was fascinated by the need that drove him on. Inside he seemed to be wrestling with himself, painfully striving to reach something elusive. Yet she did not feel alone as she did when she went to bed with Richard. This man had offered her something and now sought his own justification in return. Her glimpse of his search for fulfilment seemed to give her a brief insight into the soul whose mysteries she had first appreciated in the church porch. The experience prompted her to recall the image of the labyrinth that had struck her when she first visited the church and attended that distant memorial service. Her instinct told her that his story was also complex. But she could not turn back. He didn't look at her as he climaxed and she was left unsure as to whether he was fully satisfied.

They lay for some time, quiet and close, exchanging hardly a word. She was conscious of feeling relaxed, but of some tension in the man, and aware of the danger of spoiling this intimacy with questions. She shut her eyes.

When she awoke, Anna stepped away from the couch. His eyes were closed and he seemed to be dozing still. Anna left the room to find two clean towels and, placing one on the couch beside him, went to take a shower.

She felt no guilt over what had happened, and no fear, and whilst acknowledging to herself the potential folly of her action, felt only a sense of peace. She realised how much she had needed to communicate her frustration. She slowly dressed and dried her hair. There was still no sign of movement from the study. Then the bell rang. It was an old-fashioned mechanical bell system that announced a presence as much as requesting entry. Anna had not been aware of anyone coming up the drive and the sound of the bell jolted her into a spasm of panic. She was acutely aware of the unlocked front door. She looked through the study door to where her lover was still lying on the couch, but with the towel wrapped around him, suddenly alert.

"There's someone at the front door," she said, and abruptly closed the study behind her. As she crossed the hall the bell rang again, insistently. She looked guiltily at herself in the mirror and opened the door.

The rector was standing in the porch, carrying the baskets which she had abandoned at the site of the shrine.

'I'm just returning these, with our grateful thanks,' he said. 'The displays are very beautiful, Anna, and will be much appreciated... as always.'

'I was coming back for them later, but thank you for bringing them over,' she replied. Her mind's eye could not stop running the film of her recent encounter, and she wondered whether the rector knew that she'd just had sex.

'You'd left them in the churchyard,' he added. She blushed and then wondered whether he'd actually seen her leave with... with who? She still didn't even know his name. Suddenly she felt vulnerable.

'Where shall I put these?' he asked, stepping into the hall.

'I'll take them,' she said, putting out her hands.

'Is everything alright, Anna?' he enquired.

She didn't know how to answer.

When the rector left she found that she was trembling all over. The shock had stirred her and she now felt that she wanted to be left alone to absorb the impact of what had happened. She went through the kitchen into the garden and consciously avoided looking in the direction of the study window. The intrusion of the rector had stolen her confidence. An inner urgency had led her to direct the affair but now that certainty had left her. She had no notion of time. Finally she did turn towards the window and saw the man watching her, intent as was his manner. A moment or two later he hesitantly joined her outside. He was fully dressed and seemed to have caught her changed mood.

They looked at each other, and he appeared to be waiting for her to make some sort of decision. She sensed a disappointment in her inability to continue to dictate the course of events. That connection between them had somehow been lost. He looked away, frowning, tense. There was an unspoken chasm between them and she didn't know how to deal with it.

'I should go now,' he said, finally.

She nodded. Still she felt unable to speak. It was as if the risky intimacy that had taken place, both at the church and on the study couch, had left her totally exposed. In his turn he seemed uncertain. But Anna also sensed an unexpressed frustration and a shade of underlying anger aroused by the apparent inadequacy of her own responses. She sensed a danger in the man and in the situation.

'How long will you be staying here?' she said at last.

He made a sound that Anna could not interpret but which seemed to further reinforce the barrier that was coming between them. Then, quietly and quite deliberately, he replied, 'I don't know.' It seemed to Anna as if he were travelling far away, to the place where he'd been when she first encountered him in the church porch.

'I don't even know where you're staying,' she said, aware that, more importantly, she didn't even know who he was.

'I told you I was camping,' he said. He hadn't, she thought.

'I might come by and find you,' she replied.

Almost reluctantly he went on, 'I'm staying at Maidenhill Farm.'

'But that's where the accident happened,' Anna blurted out and then bit her lip. She felt embarrassed that she should reveal her continuing preoccupation with that long-ago event.

'I know,' he replied. 'Spooky, isn't it.' He laughed a humourless laugh.

Anna felt very cold although the sun still held the warmth of a bright Easter late afternoon.

He went on, almost speaking to himself. 'I'll definitely stay until Monday.'

They stood silently for a moment or two longer in the quiet garden. Anna did not want him to go back into the house. 'There's a way through there,' she said, pointing to the gate, feeling slightly sick as she spoke. She wanted him to leave.

Abruptly the man turned away and walked out of the garden without looking back. Anna felt an enormous sense of relief mixed with an acute disappointment in herself. Why had she allowed this momentous episode to be left so incomplete? Why had her glorious sense of strength degenerated so pitifully following the intrusion of the rector? It was almost as if her image of her own behaviour had become tarnished when she was reminded of her tributes and of the sanctity of the young couple. Their image rose before her more strongly than ever. She saw their picture as she had memorised it from newspaper cuttings – trusting, optimistic, a shy pride in being photographed together. She had never met them and yet they were more real to her now than the man she had just made love to. He had become a ghost.

And Richard, where was his place in this picture of her world? He seemed to belong elsewhere, in another reality, another life almost. The stranger, ghost as he seemed, was more connected to her through the intensity of their lovemaking and an instinctive empathy with her spiritual interests. This included his passive understanding of her obsession with the young couple. But of course they would not be young now. Anna knew just how much she had transfixed them in one time and place. The truth was that she had grown and they had remained the same, as they were at twenty-one, twenty-two, only six years younger than she had been at the time of their death. They only seemed so much younger because she knew them through words, through out-of-date photographs and romantic images. Thirteen years ago the age difference between them at that time would have seemed momentous.

Consciously pulling herself from her reverie she went inside, and then thoughtfully locked the front door of the cottage. Then she opened the door of her study and picked up the towel which she had given her visitor and which had been neatly folded and placed over the back of her writing chair. She picked it up and smelt him on it. Something of him remained alive in that room, the smell lingering, sharp, whilst something of his actual presence still seemed shadowy. Perhaps the fact that she had no name for him made him seem more phantasmic. She wondered about his age. She had assumed that they were peers and yet... he might be anything from thirty-five to forty-five. Anna was also conscious of an anomaly, of a sense of something unanswered which she couldn't quite get to grips with. She sat down on the study couch and slowly went over the events of the day. In reliving her passion Anna became aware of how much she had been turned on by the situation rather than the man. She had opened, spontaneously, given the opportunity to share herself and given an uncritical response to her openness. It had felt ordained. And now her thoughts were interrupted by an insistent inner voice. *How did he know that the fire had happened at Maidenhill Farm?* She could not remember sharing that detail. Perhaps he had made an assumption. But he spoke of it with a certainty of knowledge. She wanted to question him, to find out whether he knew more about the tragedy than he had revealed. Had he examined material in her study while she'd left him to make the coffee, or later whilst she was having a shower, or walking in the garden? This new sense of his possible deception, his secrecy, was disturbing and increasingly made her feel insecure. She almost wanted to walk up to Maidenhill Farm there and then to confront him.

Then the telephone rang.

Anna let it ring. She could not answer. She did not know what she would say to Richard if he was on the phone. It couldn't be her lover, he didn't have her number, but something inside her still believed it might be him, somehow able, mysteriously, to contact her. 'Witches,' he had said. What made him think of that? Strange that psionics featured so strongly in her half completed book. She didn't yet know what she wanted to say to him when they did speak again, or how she might ask the question that burned to be asked. But she knew that she did want to see him again, potentially to further consummate the passion that had flared so abruptly that afternoon. Through that she sensed she would regain the strength she'd felt and a new sense of completeness. She would go and see him tomorrow, but in the meantime she let the telephone keep ringing.

Anna rose to shut out the enveloping darkness. It was as if the combination of ringing telephone and exposed window might allow the caller, whoever it was, to see inside the room. When the phone stopped ringing she then felt panicked by the abrupt silence. Decisively she picked up the coffee tray from her study desk and took it back to the kitchen. Then, with a deliberately measured pace, she walked around the cottage, locking windows and doors.

In her bedroom she realised with a shock that she felt that she belonged in this cottage alone. Richard did not live there. He had the status of an occasional visitor. She felt that she could not have let him in if he'd returned at that moment.

Once these precautions were complete Anna returned to the study. The sense of potential deception was strong and she sought to identify any change in the room which might confirm whether her friend had explored her things, her books or her work. The reference and research material on her desk, some of it featuring psychic phenomena, had certainly been examined. But she knew that anyway because he'd been openly looking at the books when she came back from the kitchen. Her latest handwritten notes lay in a folder, apparently undisturbed. Her attention wandered over the bookshelves, variously dotted with picture postcard images, magazine cuttings and occasional reference notes. All her carefully collected references to the camping tragedy were preserved separately, kept in a private box in the right-hand drawer of her desk. It was as if she had buried this collection out of sight to prove to Richard that it was no longer of interest to her. The drawer was not kept locked, it had seemed sufficient that she had taken the material from view, made a commitment as it were to stop revisiting this poignant past of which Richard disapproved. She opened the drawer.

Anna lifted the box of memorabilia as something precious. It was not that long since she had last looked inside but it was a long time since she'd been through the contents in detail. She examined the material with a thrill of recognition, akin to revisiting the tokens of a former, cherished love affair. Anna kept the box as she had kept private souvenirs as a child, magic mementoes that could be taken out and held in secret, with a meaning held only for her. The press cuttings, and photocopies of cuttings, were familiar to her as was the Order of Service for the memorial event in which she and Richard had unwittingly participated. Included in the collection were her photographs of the church and the decorated shrine. She had recorded the latter each year, with her own floral tribute. There were also photographs of Maidenhill Farm and the camping field, and a large-scale ordnance survey map of the immediate area. Anna stared at the map, feeling the same coldness that she had experienced earlier, in the garden before the man had left. There was no question: the map had been opened. It had not been refolded correctly.

Anna felt her face redden with shame. The stealthy opening of her desk, presumably whilst she was in the shower – or was it while she was in the garden? – made her feel defenceless. Then she saw that he'd also taken something.

There had been an original cutting from a local weekly paper, passed on by someone who had been there at the time, a cutting that recorded the double funeral. This had gone. Anna knew the piece well. There were photographs, a summary of the events of that Easter Saturday afternoon, a eulogy for the young couple, described as "so much in love", and a journalistic attempt to wrap up the tragedy as far as the impact on the local community was concerned.

Anna replaced her box in the desk and this time locked the drawer.

She sat silently on the floor of her study, conscious still of the stale smells of sex and of the man that she had coupled with earlier. There were too many unanswered questions for her to go comfortably to bed. Aside from the events of that day, many of them concerned her time with Richard and her life over the last twelve years. But the questions also went back longer, to her own youth and childhood; to decisions that she had taken and not taken as a young woman; and to the shape of her life to come.

Anna slept fitfully on the couch in the study, experiencing short bursts of dream, snatched between the vivid, semi-real daydreams of half waking.

In the morning Anna felt as if she had experienced a ferocious night on the town, leaving her with a dense headache and an inability to move. The study now seemed to be her only remaining sanctuary. She wondered if this were like the impact of a breakdown, the sense that all courage to face human interaction and all strength to renew contact with the world had been irretrievably lost.

She recalled one vivid fantasy of the night before. It involved the young man who had burnt to death. She had visited him in his tent. The girl was not there. He remained the person from the press cuttings, fresh and unformed. She was as now, older, unsure and sad. She had sought comfort from him, initially as if he were a fortune teller or spiritual guru, and then more directly as a man. She had spewed out, in short bursts, between moments of intense physical passion, the story of her unhappiness. It was as if she had been able to give him everything, draining herself of all privacy. But she had known nothing of him. He had remained enigmatic. Then, the girl had returned. She had caught them, naked, covered in juices, exposed in the excesses that had taken place. There was nothing that could be said, no means of atonement. The girl was breathing so hard that Anna was only conscious of the hoarse roar of her breath. By contrast there was no reaction from the boy, he remained calm and almost saint like in his resignation. Then, as if in slow motion, Anna saw, apparently from a distance, that the girl had seized the small calor gas burner at the tent entrance and was directing the contents as if spraying air freshener into the pollution of the tent. The girl flicked a lighter. In the split second of the explosion Anna saw the light of experience, responsibility and pain on the boy's face, before it blackened and melted in front of her eyes.

The impact of chinks of sunlight streaming in through the study window gradually eased the worst of the night's tension. Anna slowly began to recover some poise and to ridicule the anxiety that had gripped her when she first awoke. She wryly contemplated the reaction of the man she'd met yesterday in the event that she revealed this latest response to the long-dead village tragedy. She somehow felt as if there would be the same wondering, non-committal look.

Then she began to doubt whether he had, after all, taken the press cutting from her drawer.

Perhaps she had removed it herself and placed it elsewhere, or – was it even possible that Richard had snooped in her study? But why would Richard remove the cutting? Why should the man remove the cutting for that matter? She realised how much her absorption with the camping accident was becoming a focus for all her other anxieties. Anna determined to walk up to Maidenhill Farm, to relieve the uncertainties that were flooding her mind.

She was familiar with the camping field. It had occasional use from late March, though activity was mainly focused in the summer. She had walked past the site on many occasions. With the field entrance close to the farm buildings Anna was always conscious of the likelihood of being recognised. Today, with the urgency of her need to visit, that sensitivity no longer seemed to matter.

She had expected the field to be nearly empty. She had not anticipated that there would only be one tent and that it would be pitched almost exactly where, as she understood it, the accident had taken place. A tingling of her fear from the night before gripped Anna once again. As she cautiously stepped across the field she was aware of the dew from the grass soaking her legs. The discomfort of her wet jeans intruded upon her desire to focus her thoughts and determine what she wanted to say.

The tent was small and looked worn. '*Sad really*', he'd said. There was an orange flysheet covered with beads of dew, as if the tent had been perspiring overnight. Anna had assumed that he would see or hear her coming over the field, but there was no sign or sound from within and the inner entrance was zipped shut. She stood silently in front of the tent wondering what to say.

She had not expected that he would still be asleep. Cautiously she crouched down, glimpsing the supplies carefully tucked between the inner tent and flysheet. There was a washing bowl, a water carrier, cooking equipment.

'Hi,' she said, calling through the zipped flap. 'Hi. It's me, Anna.' It sounded ridiculous, but in any case there was no response. Anna looked over her shoulder at the deserted field and the silent farm buildings beyond. Her body felt as it had when she had crouched in front of the shrine, following their meeting in the church – was it only yesterday? Decisively she took hold of the zip and opened the entrance of the tent. There was a mosquito net barring her entry, but she could see that he wasn't there. Without speaking she unzipped the second layer.

Kneeling into the tent Anna examined the interior, which was orderly but surprisingly full. Although a temporary refuge, it was one where somebody intended to spend some time.

The bedding looked comfortable and deep. There was a large rucksack, smothered in pockets, placed carefully in the bell end. Around the edge of the bedding were neatly assembled piles, comprising newspapers, folded clothes, books, writing materials and notebooks. There was a photograph album placed near the pillows. It reminded Anna of her study.

Once again she looked behind her across the deserted field. There was no sign of the man. The clouds had covered the early morning sun and she shivered, acutely conscious of her dampness and the discomfort of holding wet shoes above the soft, dry bedding material. Pulling off her trainers and leaving them on the grass outside, Anna rolled up her jeans and sat into the tent, zipping the mosquito net shut. The duvet felt inviting to her bare feet. Then she saw the cutting.

It had been placed underneath one of the notebooks, but though half concealed she recognised it immediately. To make sure, she lifted the book and opened the press cutting. She read the familiar story, which seemed to take on new meaning absorbed in the very place where the tragedy had occurred. She wanted to speak the words aloud and to hear them echoed back, to experience the connection. Then Anna looked at the photographs. As well as portraits of the young people there was an image from the joint family funerals, mourners arriving, friends, family, acquaintances, and tears being shed. In that picture Anna saw a face that she now recognised. It was the face of the man that she had met and in whose tent she was sitting.

So that explained why he had taken it. Or did it? Did he want the cutting because he was part of the story, or had he taken it to prevent her from knowing that? Anna sat and tried to absorb the implications of her discovery. Above all she wondered about his pain, that he was unable to share his involvement. She read the caption and, at last, knew his name.

Carefully, as if in a museum, Anna reached out to the photograph album placed, almost as if on display, at the side of the pillow. It did not surprise her to find that the photographs were old, thirteen or more years at least. Many of them were already fading, with colours that were degenerating under the tacky plastic of the album leaves. They were images that Anna had not seen before, living images it almost seemed, of the young couple whose faces she knew so well. It was like rediscovering them afresh, seeing facets of personality that had not shone through the portraits she had seen to date.

One image in particular held her attention. The couple were sitting outside, at a café table, hands entwined on the tabletop. The girl was looking at the camera – or was it at the photographer – with what seemed like a secretive expression of flirtatious delight. Her eyes seemed to search the lens. In the window of the café behind her could be seen the reflection of the photographer himself, face behind the camera, but unmistakably the reflection of

Anna's companion of the day before. That image was the only one in the album in which any person appeared other than the couple themselves. The photographer was anonymous, apart from in that one moment. Mostly the two were in shot together, nearly always touching, hands held, arms interlinked or wrapped. Occasionally there was a frame of one or other of them on their own. Anna had a feeling that all the pictures were taken within one short period of time – perhaps during a holiday they had taken together.

She refolded her newspaper cutting and without quite knowing why replaced it under the notebook. Then, after a moment's hesitation, and after listening intently for any sign of the man returning, she opened the notebook. Briefly, and almost unconsciously, she memorised exactly where the book was lying.

It was written in a female hand, which Anna had not expected, and copiously illustrated with ink drawings and quotations. The drawings included caricatures of faces and of figures. There were verses that read like spells, with quotations about necromancy. In addition this was a journal, with diary entries which showed absolutely that this was the writing of the young girl who had died. Why had the man been recipient of this? Had it been given to him, or had he taken it. In addition to entries that spoke of time spent with the boy, capturing something of their relationship, the journal moved effortlessly into superficial exploration of second-sight and the paranormal. This read like someone playing and dabbling, showing an immaturity, but also an arrogant certainty of knowledge that Anna found distasteful. There was an unpleasant confidence in the conclusions that were being drawn. She stopped flicking through pages when she recognised an ink portrait of the man she had come to see. It was a perceptive drawing, exaggerating the intensity of the man. But there was also much cruelty in the style of the illustration. Written alongside the image were the words 'desperate in love' with three exclamation marks. There were other comments, childish and rather brutal. Anna felt betrayed by this mockery, betrayed in her previously held idealistic view of the girl. She wondered if her feelings were as a result of bitterness from her own loss of confidence and creative urge. Perhaps she had herself felt this same certainty, and had the same arrogance at this young age. Or was she simply feeling empathy for the man she had been intimate with, sympathising with his unreturned feelings for the girl who used them for her own pleasure in her diary? Behind each entry Anna was conscious of the image of the girl, in the picture outside the café, slyly revealing some furtive intimacy with the photographer.

There was no doubt that pleasure in her relationship with the boyfriend also spilled from the diary, but to Anna it seemed a self-indulgent love, with little reference to the person that she caressed so publicly in the holiday photographs. It was self-absorbed. Anna was distressed by the dislike she now felt for this personality. Together the album and journal brought reality into the open, tarnished.

Anna was jolted once again by the images from her dream, especially the face of the girl as she spewed inflammable gas into the tent. Her imagination started leading her into new and previously unexplored territory. She pulled herself back to the reality of the moment.

The man had chosen to come here for the anniversary, all these years later. Why? He must have known about the stone in the churchyard. Had he deliberately pitched his tent in the exact location where they met their death? But from her diary the girl did not seem worthy of feelings that were still raw thirteen years later. Had he, like Anna, created an image that was a fantasy, out of the sheer horror of the events that had occurred?

Amongst the writing materials at the side of the bed were some sheets torn from a pad. They appeared to be rough jottings and notes, and Anna had ignored them at first. Now she picked them up. She saw that the writing was recent, the framework of a poem. The words were carefully chosen, stimulated by a sexual encounter, possibly the experience with Anna herself. They aroused her. Compared with the girl's journal the feelings had the sense of being wrung out, rather than held up for display. There was a hard-fought intensity, with an imagery that was savage. There had, it seemed, been a bloody fight to extract the language. At the end of the poem, or draft of a poem, the language softened to expose a poignant expression of love that touched Anna deeply. It was clear that whilst the experience of the day before may have been the catalyst, the intensity was not for Anna but for a long-lost love, a love that she had somehow been responsible for evoking. Anna was moved that she should have revived long-suppressed feelings. She saw his face as he came in love, struggling to control a passion that had once existed and had been snatched, and left unfulfilled.

Then she heard footfalls in the silence of the field and knew that he'd returned.

There was a pause and an unnatural silence. No time for her to replace that which she shouldn't have seen. She somehow felt as if she mustn't move or make a noise. She could see his form through the mosquito net, and then the score of the zipper scorched through her body and he was looking in at her, revealed. For the first time she was able to call him by his name.

There was a long silence as he drank in the implications of her discoveries. It seemed as if there was an exchange of knowledge, like telegraphic transfer. She remembered again his murmur of 'witches'. There was nowhere that either could hide. As he came into the tent he carefully zipped both the outer and inner door shut. Sitting, he meticulously held his boots above the bedclothes and slowly unlaced them. Then he removed his coat, taking a freshly purchased box of matches from the pocket and placing it on top of the books at the side of the tent.

'They used to burn them,' he said at last. 'Witches,' he added.

Anna felt as if her chest was going to burst.

'How much do you know?' he went on.

'I don't know,' she struggled to respond, 'at least – I don't understand.'

'It's simple,' he said. 'I killed them.'

To Anna the whole tent seemed to be dislocating, the ground disappearing from beneath her as if she was on a boat. She could hear her own voice repeating 'no, please, no,' and the man sobbing, a deep drawn-out sob, that sounded as if it was sucked from the ocean floor, before he clutched her and held her tight. They would drown together.

It was sometime later that thick, black smoke was seen coming from the camping field.

By the time help reached the lonely tent, strung in the damp Easter field like something unwanted, it was a tent no more. Bright orange fragments floated to the ground and checkered the blackened debris of nylon, cotton, paper and melted metal. The inferno had left a smouldering rubbish tip from which half-burnt shreds fluttered in the slightest breeze. A blackened ring of grass surrounded the spot, like the remnants of a magic circle.

It was not until after Easter Monday that identification was able to take place. The village was much quieter in its response to this iden-tikit tragedy. It was as if any talk might bring unacceptable atten-tion, and that this small community inwardly acknowledged they harboured a secret which, if revealed, might result in a witch hunt. Nobody wished to initiate the consequences of public conjecture. If the village rector had any knowledge of the events of that weekend, then he kept them exclusively to himself.

Richard returned home on Easter Monday, unaware initially of what had happened during his absence. His first knowledge was reading an account in a national paper at a motorway service station on route. Nobody was named.

When he arrived home he found Anna in the garden. She had made a small pyre to dispose of her memorabilia from the village tragedy. Strangely she had felt a need to burn everything, all the detail. She made no reference to what had taken place over that weekend and kept locked inside her the secrets she had discovered before she left the camping field, the secrets of an unspoken passion, boy for boy, which had been ridiculed by the girl she had previously sanctified. The knowledge had allowed her to break free from her own illusory obsession, and given her the impetus to refocus her life and relationship.

For Anna there was a new life ahead, and one in which she could finally complete the novel.

There were no further Easter flower arrangements.

JEANIE

Part One

1984 – Memories written by Kit Armstrong

I STAND SHIVERING IN FRONT OF the portico at Chart Court, my feet etching prints in the sprinkling of Easter snow. It is Bob-a-Job Week and Miss Jean will be welcoming. That is, if I dare ascend the cold stairs to her top-floor flat, which will mean passing the doorway of the wicked witch, Miss Buss at Flat 2, and the Colonel's door at Flat 3. I don't know who lives in Flat 1. The inside of Chart Court glistens with the smell of the wood polish that shines the oak banisters and wood panelled stairwell. I climb quietly, on tiptoe, to avoid waking the witch. I can hear her cat mewing, the cat that she never allows out, and that feeds only on chicken breast. I could not do Bob-a-Job for Miss Buss.

Miss Jean's soft voice caresses me with a reassuring, 'Yes dear,' and, in the warmth of her manicured flat, she sets me the task of making her grate shiny black. I wonder if the black stuff can be used on shoes as well. Or maybe on her car. Miss Jean drives a black Ford Popular that is very old. It is not like other cars. It has an indicator that is a little orange flag that pops out from the side. I don't think anyone would see it. Miss Jean always signals with her arm as well, just in case. When she is turning left she swings her arm round and round. The registration number of her car is QUE 2, like Queen 2, and she calls the car Bessie. She tells me that she always looks out for the registration number QUE 1, but she has never seen it. The car is parked in the courtyard behind Chart Court, the courtyard around which is a horseshoe of trees and bushes, hiding part of the garden next door where the dog barks. One day, perhaps, Miss Jean will ask me to wash the car, but it is too big a task for Bob-a-Job. I have seen Miss Jean starting the car with a special handle. She pokes it into the engine. The spare wheel sits outside on the boot. When I visit her, Miss Jean talks to me about books. She likes to know what I've read and sometimes calls me, 'the boy next door'.

After I have completed my Bob-a-Job, Miss Jean invites me to stay for lunch. I have had lunch with her before. As always, it is salmon salad. Tinned salmon which is full of bones, with raw onion and cucumber that is overripe and repeats on me. I have to swallow without tasting, but Miss Jean is pleased. She tells me about her niece, Jean. Jean Jean. I don't understand why she's called Jean Jean, but she is the Mayor in the place where she lives. I don't think Miss Jean likes Jean Jean that much, although she doesn't say that. Jean Jean has to wear a chain, and her name now is Councillor Rowbotham. I am shown a picture of her with the chain. I hope I never have to clean that. Last year it was the Colonel's medals I had to clean and that was very hard. I don't believe he won them all. There were too many. Perhaps he collects them. I'm not going to call on him this year.

Miss Jean has very white, curly hair, a pink face, and old-fashioned glasses that are a strange shape. She is very gentle and kind. She likes to play card games and scrabble, and does voluntary work for a local charity. She walks quite slowly and sits upright with her fingers folded together. When she goes out she always places an orchid in a buttonhole in her blouse. She told me it was because her uncle had been a gardener, in a big house, and he always gave her flowers and fruit.

Miss Jean doesn't like boats because her father drowned in one.

I hear stories about Miss Jean through my parents.

She doesn't like the Highway Code either, and since they made our road into a dual carriageway she drives the wrong way down it, just for a short stretch as she leaves Chart Court, so she can take the crossover a little further on and go in the direction she prefers to the shops. Also, she likes to stop for a picnic on the hard shoulder of the motorway.

While I'm pretending to enjoy the salmon salad I look round Miss Jean's flat. Each time I visit I notice something else. She has a large sitting room which is very ordered. From the window you can see the courtyard and part of the next-door garden. It's open a little and when I lean out, and throw a little snow off the window ledge, the dog hears me and starts to bark. Its paw marks have made a pattern in the snow. I duck quickly back inside and pull the window too. The cup and saucer I am drinking tea from is light and thin. Despite the snow the sky is clear and the sun streams in and lights up Miss Jean's picture of the sea, which is hung over the mantelpiece. It is a big picture of a swelling sea with waves breaking. I don't know why she has a picture of the sea when she doesn't like boats.

I am sitting at a little table and Miss Jean sits opposite, watching me. She too drinks tea and smiles at me. Her sofa is very big and deep and when you sit on it you sink down, and it has a special smell.

There is a big dining table in the sitting room and it has a red cloth with decorated edges. On the table is an old typewriter. It looks ancient. Miss Jean sees me looking at it and smiles.

'I like writing letters,' she says, 'It's something you do when you're alone. Have you ever read *Robinson Crusoe*, dear?'

Miss Jean has friends that sometimes come to see her. When they come they stay for several days. I am invited for coffee and introduced as her "little friend". There is Harri, Ginger and Dixie. None of them seem to have real names. They call Miss Jean 'Jeanie'.

While Miss Jean is making the coffee her friends talk and I listen. Ginger is nervous about going out in the car with Jeanie. She says that the last time she stayed with her they drove the wrong way up a motorway slip road. Dixie asks Harri about her health and Harri says, 'It was cancer, dear. I saw my pathologist's report. But don't let's worry Jeanie.'

The coffee comes in a jug but Miss Jean has made hot milk for me and I only have a little coffee. The ginger biscuits are very nice. I wonder if Ginger likes them. When Dixie asks about Jean Jean becoming Mayor, Miss Jean glances at me and then says quietly, 'she comes to see me only when she wants something.' Then she adds, 'But let's be gracious.'

Miss Jean complains about the buddleia that is growing in the walls of Chart Court. 'It's very invasive,' she says, 'and nobody will take responsibility for its removal.' They talk about playing bridge and Miss Jean says she plans a whist drive whilst they are staying. She asks me if my parents would let me come.

'You play whist very well, I think,' she says.

The whist drive is in the evening. It is a couple of days yet before Miss Buss's cat is killed, but even so I will be dropped at home after the game. I can't be allowed to walk on my own. All the people are old, except me and one other boy. I am introduced to him and he is Miss Jean's great-nephew, Rupert, Councillor Rowbotham's son. He has come to stay because his mother is busy being Mayor. I think of Rupert Bear, or Rupert of Hentzau. There are twelve of us and Miss Jean has arranged four tables in her sitting room. All the tables have green tops. They are special card tables. I play and listen. Some people are newer acquaintances to Miss Jean and live nearby. Harri and Ginger talk about the hospital where they used to work, and where Jeanie worked too. None of them have husbands. None of them has children.

Miss Jean also has a nephew called Alexander. He is not Jean Jean's brother. She likes Alexander and speaks kindly of him. He is a teacher and fought in the war. Miss Jean is proud of him and he has a son called Peter, but they live a long way away. Jean Jean is not mentioned, even though her son is there and she is a Mayor, which is very important.

Jean Jean's son is not very nice. More like Rupert of Hentzau. Between rounds of the game I am supposed to play with him. He says he is bored and that since he came to stay he has nothing but old ladies for company, and they smell funny, and that he can't sleep because Miss Jean types at night.

'I think she's a spy,' he says. 'Or she's crazy. My mother thinks she's crazy.'

I ask him about his mother being Mayor, but he doesn't seem interested.

I come third in the whist drive and am given a little medal, which is very exciting. But, Jean Jean's son is not pleased and on the landing he threatens to fight me. He tells me that if I don't give him the medal he will strangle me with his mother's chain. I am frightened and it makes me wheeze. Once I start to wheeze it is difficult to stop. It gets worse and I am scared. The friends from nearby are leaving, but Miss Jean takes me into a bedroom to be quiet and to lie still, away from Jean Jean's son. Then she brings me some medicine on a spoon and gives me a florin as pocket money. The medicine is very hot in my mouth and when I swallow it the hotness goes all the way down and into my stomach. But it feels nice. Ginger looks through the door and says 'Gosh, Jeanie, whisky!' Miss Jean puts her finger to her lips. She tells me that she is going to teach me how to play bridge.

I am in trouble at home because I accepted a florin as "pocket money" from Miss Jean and because I drank whisky, though really they blame Miss Jean. I am not supposed to go back, even though they know Miss Jean wants me to play with Rupert as he is staying there alone now.

Then the witch's cat is found dead.

Hentzau is standing in the front driveway as I walk past Chart Court. He calls me and I am reluctant to go to him, but he says, 'don't you know what's happened?' It seems that Miss Buss's cat has been found hanged in the trees next to the Courtyard. Its tail has been cut off, like a trophy. Miss Buss is very upset.

'I think the Colonel did it,' says Jean Jean's son. 'He didn't like it because the cat was mewling all the time.'

Later I hear that Miss Buss has not been seen since the death of her cat. She has shut herself away to mourn. I go with Rupert into the courtyard and we hear the dog barking next door. It's a friendly bark. At school we have been reading *Animal Farm* and Sherlock Holmes. I wish I could meet the dog. I wonder why it didn't bark when the cat was killed.

One day soon afterwards, Miss Jean passes me in her car and pulls over. Other cars are hooting but she steps out and asks me how I am.

'Has the wheezing gone, my dear?' she asks. 'Perhaps you'll come and see me sometime soon.' She pauses and then she says, 'My great nephew is no longer with me. You'll be quite safe. And I did promise to teach you how to play bridge.'

I don't like to say that I have been told not to go to Chart Court, because of the whisky and the dead cat. In future when I see the Ford Popular coming I try and hide behind walls, so that I don't have to disappoint Miss Jean.

One day I hear that Miss Jean has been taken to hospital. She has fallen off a ladder whilst trying to cut down the buddleia that was growing on the walls of the flats.

One of the neighbours said, 'There was nobody living in Flat 1 at the time. The Colonel heard cries but thought it was crows. It was hours before she was found – with a broken hip, poor thing.'

They said it was very sad and that it can take a long time to recover at that age. That's what I heard. After that I didn't see Miss Jean again, not as far as I can remember, and in time new people moved into Chart Court. I don't know who they were. But I did learn to play bridge. I taught myself, and later joined a bridge club. I think Miss Jean would have been pleased.

Years later, perhaps when I came home during the university holidays, I did go into the courtyard at Chart Court, half hoping to see Miss Jean's Ford Popular. I hadn't heard anything about her for a long time. Of course it wasn't there. There was no barking from next door and I could see no sign of a dog. There was, however, a pile of assorted rubbish in a corner of the courtyard, an old chair with the springs showing, a paraffin drum and a fireguard. And there, amongst the rubbish, was an ancient typewriter. I am sure it was the same one, the one that used to sit on Miss Jean's red cloth in her sitting room, and that she wrote letters on at night.

Part Two

2012 – Notes written subsequent to the events

Gladys had been in the care home for three years; that's as far as she could remember. She said that it was as she imagined life would be in a prison, with periods of solitary confinement, the days so much the same that they blurred, and any real sense of time being lost. Gladys said that she thought she herself was in some way "lacking". She moved in a dream between her room, the lounge and the dining area, occasionally venturing into the modest landscaped garden, with its specially named legacy benches. But she never went beyond the garden.

People spoke to her occasionally, mainly the staff, often simply asking her to move elsewhere. Sometimes visitors to the home asked her questions, because they could see that she was more mobile and perhaps more able than most residents, but she struggled to respond.

In her own isolation, Gladys felt strange empathy for that other, silent, withdrawn woman who it seemed had lived in the home forever, or at least longer than most of the residents. Not even the staff knew how long "Tapper" had lived at the Emanuel Shinwell Home for the Elderly. The tapping for which she was renowned was more or less constant. Tap, tap, tap on the radiators in the corridor as she stood blankly for hours on end, or as she walked stiffly and slowly along the edge of the corridor, as if keeping in the shelter of the roadside or the hedge. Tap, tap, tap on her bedroom table, disturbing those in hearing when her door was open, or her neighbours on either side. But, most aggravatingly, even for Gladys, tap, tap, tap on the arms of the chairs and on the tables in the lounge, a consistent barrage nullifying any enjoyment to be taken from the continuously playing television. Tapper was in a closed world of her own, never receiving visitors and incapable of speech, producing only grunts and cries. She wore her spectacles with a sticking plaster over one eye and would not allow anyone to remove them. Like Tapper, Gladys also had no friends of her own, and rarely visitors, just a once-a-year attendance from her son. But Gladys watched people and she particularly watched Tapper. It was as if there was a long-standing connection.

Gladys watched people. She watched how they behaved in the dejected environment of the shabby and ill-resourced Emanuel Shinwell Home. She noticed that the staff manufactured cheery dispositions, perhaps more genuine for their favourite residents, but especially when any semblance of authority was present. She noticed that the residents were immune to the smell, the decor, and the dubious strings of grease and mucous that might be encountered on handrails and the arms of chairs. Gladys still noticed these things. She was like a silent spy, observing, noting, considering and trying to work out what it all meant. But she had no one to report to.

Tapper appeared to be immune to everything. Her only occupation consisted of inspecting the beds in those rooms whose doors were open. Occasionally she set about remaking a bed, but with little success.

Whilst Gladys herself was more or less invisible, she noticed the antagonism towards Tapper, who couldn't help but draw attention to herself owing to the continuous movement of her fingers and the drumming noise she created. This was guaranteed to annoy all within earshot. It especially annoyed visitors, tense already as a result of their dutiful visit to this unwholesome, contained world, where they would struggle, gamely at first, to converse with a fading relative. Most inhabitants, whilst confused, were not locked in the lonely world inhabited by Tapper. Gladys was increasingly glad of her own invisibility as she observed the abuse her fellow resident was subject to. Perhaps in resentment at their current status and lifestyle, some people would delight in nudging Tapper in the corridor, elbowing her out of the way, or pushing her to temporarily force her to cease the constant beat. Some would step up close to Tapper, in the dining room especially, and shout right in her face, screaming at her to stop, sometimes forcibly taking her hands and pressing them down, physically preventing the movement of her fingers, which would flutter like trapped birds under the restraint. The staff did little to intervene, other than gentle admonishment, probably because the residents' actions were a manifestation of what they would have liked to have done themselves.

Then, one day, Tapper had a visitor. Gladys watched the taxi pull up and the immaculately suited gentleman emerge with his tan leather briefcase. He came into the reception area and asked Gladys where he might find the manager. Silently Gladys led him to the office, but then the door shut her out.

Later, Gladys saw the man, accompanied by the manager, approach Tapper in the corridor. He tried to speak to her, and she stopped tapping. But then she simply looked at him blankly and her tongue lolled out of her mouth, dripping saliva. The man took a step back.

'How long has she been like this?' he asked.

'Ever since I started work here,' was the manager's reply. 'Her notes indicate she has been in an advanced stage of dementia for at least fifteen years.'

'And the other relative?' the man asked.

'We don't hear from him,' she replied.

He tried to touch Tapper, but she shrank away, no doubt anticipating another attack. The man shrugged, looked helplessly at the care home manager and left. That was that. Gladys brooded on what this meant.

She had no idea how long it was before the next visit. This time the man came back with a colleague. Tapper was sitting in the lounge, busy drumming on the arms of her chair. The well-dressed man stayed standing at a little distance. Perhaps he was afraid she would drip saliva onto his clothes, or maybe he didn't relish sitting on the stained chair that he was offered. The new man sat down, pulled his chair close to Tapper and gently took one of her hands. She stared at him with newly awakened interest. There seemed to be a fleeting moment of communication and then she looked away. He stayed for some time after the well-dressed man had gone. He had some books with him and read to Tapper from them. She did not appear to have any interest in what he was saying, but she did stop tapping. Gladys was sitting close by.

After the second man too had left, the manager sought out Gladys.

'Did you know our friend there will soon be one hundred?' she said, indicating Tapper. 'We think there should be a little celebration. A relative has come to visit her from New Zealand. I hope everyone will be kind.' Then she got up and left.

The relative from New Zealand came back, and once again Gladys was sitting close by. The man approached her. 'This lady is my great-aunt,' he said. 'She will be one hundred next week and we'd like to have a little party. Will you join us?'

Gladys paused and then nodded.

'Thank you,' he said.

She noticed he was speaking to other people too. No doubt inviting them also.

Part Three

2012 – A direct account from Kit Armstrong

I attended the party at the Emanuel Shinwell Home for the Elderly on the afternoon of 15 April 2012, the occasion being the hundredth birthday of one of its longest abiding residents. It was a beautiful, warm, sunny Easter and the residential home was overheated with the sun streaming through the curtain-less windows of the corridors and entrance hall.

I had been forwarded the invitation by a colleague, who intimated there was a potential documentary to be made. A number of media and press people had clearly been invited to celebrate with and hear the story of a centenarian who, as a former "Colossus Wren", had apparently been a key player in the WWII Bletchley Park Codebreaker team. My colleague had been informed that her story was captured in a series of detailed personal diaries that also covered a senior role in the early developmental days of the NHS.

The invitation was formally issued from the care home owner, a Mr Stanley Baldwin. The irony of a Stanley Baldwin owning the Manny Shinwell Home was not lost on me. So, I was intrigued to attend on several counts.

The arrangements on arrival were strange. I was ushered into a small and stifling reception room with a few other VIP guests and introduced to the care home manager, Jenny Bond, and the owner, Mr Baldwin, a voluble, late middle-aged man who had an appearance and persona that veered between fairground manager, stand-up comedian and car salesman. He in turn introduced his life partner, a chubby Filipino with little English, but who smiled a lot. Mr Baldwin, or Stan as he introduced himself, revealed that he himself lived in a caravan behind the home, something which he appeared rather bizarrely proud of. Guests, which included a number of people from the local press and radio, were offered a warm glass of prosecco and left to chat, rather self-consciously, either amongst themselves, or with the wife (whose name we never knew), whilst we wondered what was going to happen next. Mr Baldwin meanwhile had disappeared. But where was the birthday girl?

There was only limited prosecco, and it was getting increasingly hard to find some, when Baldwin reappeared, escorting a middle-aged man with a marked New Zealand accent. Still no sign of our hundred-year-old birthday girl. I began to wonder if perhaps she had not survived to enjoy her party. Baldwin now called for silence and gave an unorthodox welcome speech. It was clear that his motivation was self-promotion and advocacy for his care-home. He intimated, in a smarmy tone, how privileged the home was to number in its residents someone with such a distinguished past, and then revealed how little had been known about Miss Jean, owing to her suffering from severe dementia for more than fifteen years. He introduced the New Zealander, Peter Jean, great-nephew of the birthday lady.

The Emanuel Shinwell Home for the Elderly is not the place that I would have anticipated reconnecting with Miss Jean.

Could this really be *my* Miss Jean, Jeanie of Chart Court? Institutional, threadbare and busy, this was not Chart Court. It bore nothing of the genteel and well cared-for ambience of Miss Jean's former home. There was certainly no indication that residents might take part in scrabble evenings or whist drives. But the names… the great nephew… the role this Miss Jean had played in the NHS, her age, too, made it possible. I had not met Peter Jean, and in any case would have been hard pushed to recognise someone who was probably no more than early twenties when I was visiting his great-aunt at Chart Court. I wondered if Jean Rowbotham or Rupert were going to appear as well. However, looking round I saw nobody who appeared to match the other great-nephew, from my memory as a child. I felt a little wheeze in my chest, the first time for some years, and I shuddered in recalling my encounter with him on the day when Miss Buss's cat met its untimely end.

Peter Jean uneasily introduced himself to the assembled guests and indicated that he wanted to share a little about the celebration before we went through to join his great-aunt and the other residents in the lounge. Well, she was clearly still alive.

'Do you know what other anniversary it is today?' Mr Jean asked us, 'as well as the hundredth birthday of my great-aunt?'

No one knew, of course.

'Well, it's exactly one hundred years ago today that the *Titanic* sank. My great-great-uncle was a steward on the boat, and he died that morning, having, we understand, helped passengers safely into the lifeboats. My great-aunt was born in England the day her father died, and her knowledge of his selfless assistance to others continuously informed her own work and life. As you are all aware, as an adult Miss Jean was a Colossus Wren. She gave unstinting service to the war effort at Bletchley, where her role is unclear, partly because her integrity in honouring the Official Secrets Act means that she did not share any detailed information from that time. However, so deep-rooted were her experiences, that even today she is often found tapping code on surfaces wherever she sits. Whilst her memory has gone, the embedded skills remain, almost like a form of automatic writing. Sadly, this has been a trial to many of her peer residents, but we hope that now they know of her past heroism they will be empathetic. I hope that somewhere inside her, my great-aunt will know that she is the focus of this celebration today, though I have to warn you that she is not able to speak to you.

Having come back to England for the first time for twenty years, partly motivated by this centenary, I was determined we should mark the occasion and the significant achievements of this remarkable lady. Immediately after the war, and her role at Bletchley, she joined the emerging NHS, and took up a nursing career that ultimately led to her becoming matron of a major inner-city hospital. I know all this because I am lucky enough to be the recipient of Miss Jean's diaries, diaries that she passed on to me when I left this country for New Zealand. The contents tell a remarkable story.

I wanted to share this context with you as our important guests today. Now, I hope that Mr Baldwin and his team will allow us to join the Emanuel Shinwell residents in the lounge for a birthday tea.'

There was applause. I was certain now that I was about to re-encounter my Miss Jean. I wondered if, despite everything, it was remotely possible she might recognise me.

For the celebration, the lounge of the Emanuel Shinwell Home had been styled to create the crude ambience of a cruise ship entertainment venue. There was a semi-permanent bar in one corner with a dazzling array of spirit bottles, bar cloths and beer mats, clearly the pride and joy of Mr Baldwin. A temporary stage had been erected at one end of the lounge, and the bar-style tables and low ceiling contributed to the atmosphere, which was made pungent by cigarette smoke (surely not permissible now?) wafting from the nicotine-stained fingers of a number of residents. They clutched what appeared to be complimentary packs of Players cigarettes. Out of place were the institutional high-backed chairs, with wide arms that enabled immobile limbs to grasp and lever support. The staff were in attendance, wearing party hats and clutching glasses brimful of gin or Bacardi, posing as tap water. Frank Sinatra was playing loudly from an old-fashioned turntable.

Peter Jean wore an embarrassed expression. I watched him weave through the assemblage to the window, where a figure stood, back to the room, arm jiggling and fingers tapping on a waist-high radiator shelf. He carefully took the jiggling arm and encouraged Miss Jean to turn to the room.

In fact it is I who would not have recognised her. Her white hair was cut short and straight, very thin, with patches where there was no hair at all. The pale green dressing gown looked as if it was a second-hand hospital gown, no remnant there of the immaculate costume in which Miss Jean always prided herself. But the glasses I did remember. Those cat-eye glasses that had appeared old fashioned in my childhood had made a return, so that Miss Jean had one item of dress that was oddly current. However, the glasses had been subject to considerable wear, with one lens almost obliterated by sticking plaster which appeared to hold the spectacles together. Baldwin signalled to his staff and a tuneless rendition of 'Happy Birthday' was taken up, and spread like a wave through the crowd.

When it came to naming the recipient, there was an awkward pause and mixed response, with 'Happy birthday, dear Tapper,' clearly articulated from some parts of the room. A mobile elderly resident was ushered forward with a luxurious pot orchid, and Peter Jean presented it to his great-aunt, though she seemed disinclined to take the gift.

Urged by a distant memory I made my way across the ship's deck towards Miss Jean. It felt as if the room was swaying. Peter Jean looked at me, a little unsure, as I carefully plucked a blossom from the pot orchid and, using my tie pin, fastened it to the lapel of Miss Jean's gown.

'My great-aunt's name means *the lord is gracious*,' he said. 'I'm not sure I agree with the sentiment.'

I looked at Peter. 'I remember her from when I was a child. She gave me whisky when I was ill.'

Miss Jean looked at me sharply, then continued tapping her unknown, coded messages.

'Extraordinary. We should talk,' said Peter. 'Have you met Gladys – the lady who presented the orchid? She remembers my great-aunt from her hospital days. It's good that there are people here who value her.'

Later I sat down with Peter Jean and shared my memories. Miss Jean was standing nearby, focused on the radiator which was bearing away her tapped codes. She did not appear to be cognisant of any of our discussion. I was cautious when sharing my memory of his cousin.

'Ah, Rupert,' said Peter. 'You'll notice he is not here for the birthday celebration.'

'Are you in touch with him?' I asked.

'Briefly,' he responded. 'You may be aware that my aunt,

Rupert's mother, is no longer with us. There was some political scandal, after which her health deteriorated. I'm afraid I never got on with her. In my absence Rupert acquired Power of Attorney in the early stages of my great-aunt's oncoming dementia. Sadly, he used this to manage her assets for his own interests. That's why she is living in this place. Despite his appearance and manner, Mr Baldwin actually does care, but the resources are stretched and this is the best that her dwindling asset can sustain. I do hope you might tell her story. I was so pleased you could come, even before I realised there was a personal connection.'

'I need to read the diaries,' I replied.

'Of course. Perhaps you should talk to Rupert too,' he said. 'There may be material that was passed on to that side of the family. I'd be happy to broker a meeting.' I cautiously concurred and explained that I had changed my name to Kit, for purposes of a professional identity. He might remind Rupert that we had met as children.

I stood and carefully approached Miss Jean. I spoke to her, shared my memories of Chart Court, of her whist drives and doing Bob-a-Job. I tried calling her Jeanie. There was nothing to suggest any of these comments flickered into her consciousness. That is until I concluded by saying, 'I've read *Robinson Crusoe* now.' Then I think she briefly, momentarily connected. Her hand came forwards and clutched my arm. Then it relaxed and she returned once more to wherever her mind was now accommodated.

I sought out Gladys, who was shy but proud of her connection with Matron, as she referred to Miss Jean.

Gladys unexpectedly opened up. 'That hospital saved my life,' she said. 'I was in the cancer ward for three months. I wasn't expected to live, but Matron always ensured the place was clean and hygienic, and that the nursing staff were there when needed and knew what to do. There were no superbugs in Matron's hospital.

She even told the doctors off. She was well regarded, was Matron. And it was known her fiancé was killed in the war. On the beaches of Normandy he was killed. Not that you would have known it to look at her. People here need to have more respect.'

Four weeks later I met up with Rupert Rowbotham at a motorway service station on the M1. I had approached him using my birth name. He was driving between appointments and said it was the only convenient time he had available. Apparently he is now running a business importing botox. He revealed that previously he had been an estate agent.

Peter Jean had already shared with him my previous relationship with his great-aunt, though I didn't get any sense when we met that Rupert remembered who I was. The meeting was not helpful. Rupert either had no knowledge of any memorabilia from Miss Jean's wartime activities, or else was not prepared to share. He was irritable and disinclined to engage. However, he did come to life when I reminded him of Miss Buss's cat and how it had been found hanged.

'Oh yes,' he said. 'I remember that. I don't recall you though. I just remember some boring days staying in that antique block of flats. The woman with the cat caught me sliding down the banisters and threatened to tell my great-aunt. I got back at her by drinking the milk from her bottles, left outside her flat.'

'So, who killed the cat?' I asked. 'Do you know?'

'It wasn't killed,' he replied. 'It died. That awful woman told my great-aunt the cat had died and asked if I'd dig a hole and bury it for her in the grounds by the courtyard. She said she couldn't bear to see it being buried herself. She didn't give me anything. Look, this is terrible to admit, but as the cat was dead anyway, I made it look as if it had been hung. I suppose I just wanted to see what reaction I'd get. I was a little brat.'

'What did Miss Jean say?' I asked. 'She must have known it was you.'

'She just made me dig the hole,' he said, 'It took ages. She came out with a tape measure to make sure it was going to be deep enough. She said that otherwise dogs or foxes would dig it up again. It was hard work.'

I had to ask the question. 'How come the dog next door didn't bark? It always barked when anybody went into the Courtyard.'

'You know, I cut the cat's tail off and threw it to the dog. That kept it quiet… You need to warn Peter that the money won't last much longer,' he said. 'Once it's all gone Baldwin may not be able to keep her living in the Shinwell Home. There's probably another eighteen months left.'

That warning, though passed on to Peter Jean, who was shortly returning to New Zealand, was not needed. Shortly afterwards, during the London Olympic Games in August 2012, I was informed that Miss Jean had passed away.

Part Five

2018 – A final account from Kit Armstrong

It is now six years since Miss Jean's death.

Much as I would have liked to have made that documentary to share details of Miss Jean's life at Bletchley, and even her role in the evolving NHS, it became clear that there was no viable "story" as such. Miss Jean's extant diaries, carefully recorded on her old Underwood typewriter, covered the period 1947 to 1955 and her role in the NHS, nothing before – and nothing to betray her signing of the Official Secrets Act 1939. There was no other material to draw from. It is difficult to imagine the soft, kindly lady of Miss Jean's retirement years as the formidably efficient, senior NHS manager, overseeing a significant hospital institution. It is clear that she was a highly skilled administrator and an effective supervisor of people, probably with an aura of infallibility. The diary is primarily unemotional, though there are references by name to her friends of later years, including Harri, Ginger and Dixie. No diaries survived from post-1955, though I'm sure she was still writing when I remember her at Chart Court. I sense that she destroyed the more personal journals before she gifted her story to Peter Jean at the point when he left for New Zealand. His emigration in 1990 followed the death of his father, who had been Miss Jean's fond nephew.

There are no personal references to Alexander or to Jean Jean in the diaries. There are, however, some oblique references to Miss Jean's personal life and state of mind. She mentions asking Joe for advice, and considering how Joe would respond, how he would react to a particular issue or crisis. She also notes, somewhat wistfully, that Joe is a taboo subject for her friends. She clearly suffered the burden of grief from her fiancé's death with little or no support from others. She showed a resigned understanding that there would not be another Joe, and he remained a living presence in her day-to-day life.

In the garden at the Emmanuel Shinwell Care Home a bench is now located with a memorial plaque to Miss Jean. It reads *Miss Jean 'Jeanie'. Rest in Peace. We all have our time, and are then forgotten. The Lord is Gracious.*

Peter Jean kindly let me help him determine the wording.

I still don't know how Miss Jean managed to get the registration number for her old Ford Popular - QUE 2.

THE BOARDER

M Y BROTHER DIED TODAY.
The call came after midnight. I was already in bed,
dreaming about Stefan.

Stefan and I meet by chance, in the park. He looks older and his
blond hair is thinner so that his scalp is visible. He recognises his
old friend and tells me how he's spending his time. He is still lean
and I gather he walks a lot. But intellectually he's not able to do
much. He is a loner, unable to concentrate enough to work. Still,
Stefan is alive.

My heart was racing as I sat up in bed with the phone ringing by
my side. As I absorbed the news in my sharply woken state, the
song started in my head…

I know you've deceived me, now here's a surprise…

and I was transported back forty years, to the first time I heard that
song, the sound coming from the radio through the flimsy parti-
tion from my older brother's bedroom.

I was transported back to school, and to the notice board of sales and wants with the advert that jumped out a mile: *Single for sale, 'I Can See for Miles' 2 shillings. Meet here Wednesday morning break.* My brother's birthday was coming up. He didn't have a record player, but he wanted the record. At that time he was my hero. No other boy mattered. Until Stefan, that is.

At Wednesday morning break Stefan was there. He was also older than me. There was no one else waiting. He said he had to sell the record because he was a boarder; the school was closing its boarding facility and he had to sell his possessions. It didn't quite make sense. Nevertheless, I followed him upstairs through corridors previously unseen and places where he said we needed to go carefully, as boarders were not allowed there in the daytime.

In the long, sparse dormitory we stopped by his bed and he retrieved the record from a plastic sleeve. He said he was keeping that. I gave him a shiny two-shilling piece. I fell in love with him instantly.

'Do you like it? *There's magic in my eyes,*' he drawled, and laughed. 'I want to see the Eiffel Tower and the Taj Mahal one day,' he said, and then he added, 'Just like the song,' in case I didn't know the lyrics.

I watched him after that, when I saw him around school, or when I could get down to the ever-muddy playing fields, often in the rain, and see him representing the school team at football or cricket. He was good. And he started to notice me, in a fond, patronising sort of way. Sometimes he'd speak. We were building a relationship. I did see him socially, from time to time, at parties or special events where lots of people came together. There was always something there between us, but we didn't "go out" together. We couldn't go out together. Not then. And in any case, as long as we were friends there was no danger of the song coming true…

You took advantage of my trust in you when I was so far away…

I think my brother was pleased with the record, but he didn't say very much. And of course he couldn't play it, not then anyway. I wasn't bothered because by then the record, for me, was more about Stefan than it was about him.

It is hard to believe it is now forty years since I heard that song. Over the years Stefan has drifted in and out of my life. Although I have found another relationship, there is still some intimacy between us when we meet. I see him at least once a year, maybe more often.

Of course things were different after his illness. He was no longer able to play sport, at least not at the same level. And whereas before he had been confident, almost arrogant, after getting ill Stefan seemed to withdraw into himself and to live at a pace that was slightly less hurried than everyone else, as if he had all the time in the world. And in a way he did, because he didn't seem to have a purpose; it was as if he was waiting to be told what the meaning of his life was.

We talked more each time we met and he was very philosophical. He was glad to be alive, to be well. That was enough. Most of the time we seemed to meet by accident, but just occasionally we did arrange to meet and that gave me a thrill, even after all those years. I suppose I was still in love with him in a way.

My brother died today.

The call came after midnight when I was already in bed, dreaming about Stefan.

My heart was racing as I sat up with the phone ringing by my side. I knew instantly. It was my father, calling to tell me. His long illness was over. He had lasted a lot longer than Stefan did.

Maybe it was the shock of waking to the phone and knowing instinctively what the news would bring. I don't know. But this was the first time I realised that for nearly forty years I had been dreaming Stefan's ongoing life. He had disappeared towards the end of his final term, and it was a while before it became known he was ill…

I know you've deceived me, now here's a surprise…

Then I had a phone call, through school, to say he'd like to see me. It was a surprise. I didn't stay long, his parents were there, but there was a sense that it was special to be invited. They told me not to expect him to recover. I didn't see Stefan again, and I didn't go to his funeral. Was I invited? I wish I had gone. Instead I dreamed about him, for years, living out his life as if it was ongoing, in my dreams.

I can see for miles and miles and…

THE RAILWAY CLOCK

1

H OLLAND FOUND THE RAILWAY CLOCK tucked inside a discoloured cardboard box in the corner of the attic.

The clock was resting, unwound and overlooked, in a nest of ancient, crumpled sheets of newspaper. He felt as if he had opened an Egyptian tomb.

For several minutes Holland knelt on the rafters and stared at his find before lifting it carefully from the paper cocoon. With this gentle movement the mechanism of the railway clock (though he didn't think of it this way until later) recommenced and it momentarily ticked. The sound was rich and attractive. He carefully replaced the clock in its box and took it downstairs.

Holland positioned it like a prize exhibit in the centre of his kitchen table, on the rich, orange, chenille cloth he'd inherited from his mother. The clock was only about eight inches high, a Victorian carriage clock with a case made from polished oak, but it was somehow dense and imposing.

He was a cautious man. He unfolded each crumpled sheet of newspaper and examined them carefully. The sheets were not from a single edition but bore several dates during the early 1930s.

Holland smoothed out leaders that highlighted economic and political crisis – rising unemployment figures, sterling devaluation, fall of the Labour Government, rise of Nazism, and later the onset of the Spanish Civil War. There was nothing else in the box. He tentatively lifted the clock and a lighter, back panel dropped away to reveal the intricate mechanism and a decorative brass winding key which clung to a tiny metal peg. A square piece of curling, gummed paper was stuck to the inside of the fallen panel. On this was handwritten, in barely decipherable black ink, *clock case made of oak taken from the viaduct of the Great Western Railway, demolished 1889.*

He wanted to keep it.

The railways were in Holland's blood. As a child he had been held rapt by the final days of steam and as a young adult, when others were exploring Teddy Boy culture and the beginnings of rock, he was obsessed with (and dismayed by) Beeching. He spent many solitary hours on station platforms with the railways his focus of energy and activity. He joined British Rail, where an undistinguished career as a crossing keeper flew past like a second-run Flying Scotsman. His career culminated in junior middle management, with a frustrating period following privatisation, and with early retirement after the advent of Network Rail.

Holland's life was uneventful. He remained unmarried, supported his mother after his father's early death, attended occasional family events and social nights at the local club, and from time to time wondered what he might do with his life. Now he preserved his un-exceptional collection of railway memorabilia as a last link with his childhood passion. The clock seemed like a gift from the railway gods.

Since his mother's death, Holland had moved into the unreasonably large Victorian villa which he had bought at auction on a whim that summer. Passing the run-down, empty-for-sale property, he had spotted an unobtrusive "Do not trespass on the railway" sign on the gate through to the back garden. Irresistibly drawn, he had returned in a fever of indecision before timidly visiting the agent and obtaining a viewing.

Even then he might not have succumbed, but the agent being required elsewhere, left him to wander alone in the house and garden for nearly an hour. In the rear garden, that was dank with moss and rotting wood, and wildly overgrown, he discovered the platform bench and Great Western Railway gate. In the comforting seclusion of the lonely garden and the warmth of a bright early summer's day, Holland finally decided on his life's purpose – to create his own railway museum.

The railway clock remained on Holland's table in the room that he called the scullery, leading to the kitchen. After winding it the clock told time inaccurately and the hands moved without any apparent logic.

He meant to consult his solicitor, to check rights of possession and to seek information, from the property deeds, about previous owners of the villa. He understood that the property had been compulsorily purchased by the Council prior to the auction. It had been empty and untended for many years, which explained why he'd been able to afford it. In the meantime he had more pressing missions – to trace the original local lines of the Great Western Railway, "God's Wonderful Railway", and its viaduct, in the late 1880s; and to evict the children whom he had found were creating dens in the wilder parts of his museum garden.

When he had moved into the house in early autumn, Holland had realised that all his resources were going to be needed to simply make it fully habitable. Sadly, he was not going to be left with the capital to properly initiate his museum project. Instead, he foresaw a considerable body of work for himself in clearing the garden and uncovering the railway memorabilia. It was in assessing the work required that he had become aware that he shared his outdoor space with others.

It had taken him some time to get his bearings outside, to understand the connections between the overgrown pathways, how to find the middle lawn, where the extent of the plot ended, and the position of the boundaries with neighbouring properties. On each expedition into the heart of the garden he would discover new features and landmarks. A wondrous find had been on opening the large shed, almost completely obliterated by climbing ivy, the vegetation so thick it had prevented access. Once he had cleared the doorway and made his way inside, he found the building was actually a former railway station ticket office. Despite being piled high with old tins and boxes, the counter and screen were still in place, and there were wall-mounted metallic notices giving information and instructions. This further confirmed the decision he had taken to purchase the house. He felt as if he was starting to own the space.

He never saw those who came into the garden, but he heard them. Sometimes at the weekend there were sounds of laughter and running. Occasionally, at night, he saw the glow of cigarettes and even, once, a small fire. He found the remains of the activity that had taken place and two or three carefully hollowed-out areas in shrubs and bushes that were regular haunts and homes to his weekend and nocturnal visitors, who he now assumed were teenagers.

2

When the letter arrived, it was addressed to 'The Occupier', in a handwritten light blue envelope which, for some reason, made Holland feel uneasy. The envelope smelt stale and he hesitated before opening it.

In a short and touching note the writer spoke of having lived in the house some time before and of being anxious to revisit their old home. They would be in contact to propose a date and time and hoped that would be acceptable. Holland could not read the signature and, as no further details were given, he was not able to respond to the request.

A troubling feeling of insecurity now intruded on Holland's life and he delayed continuing his planned railway research. He didn't know what to expect from his correspondent. His newly purchased computer, with which he was just starting to feel confident, provided a research route that could satisfy his curiosity about the origins of the railway clock, or at least the viaduct from which it had been made. However, restless and unsettled, he was slow to test his new-found computer skills, and he felt blocked in his aspirations.

In an attempt to conquer this frustration he did, however, take a long-handled rake and set about exorcising the various dens that pockmarked his proposed museum garden. He both resented and was disturbed by the invasions into his space.

The visits brought back uncomfortable childhood memories of his own, of being mocked by other children and young people who played within the confines of his father's property, or rather within the railway property that his father maintained, being a sta-tionmaster with a tied house and garden. He recalled his surprise at his father's rage in response to the trespassing. In retrospect Holland realised that his father's reaction was more to do with the property invasion than with the bullying of his son. Nevertheless, he enjoyed a feeling of smugness as he tore down the dens and removed the evidence of the intruders' activities.

Afterwards he felt exhausted. He was more aware than ever of the extent of work required to create his museum. He had also found more than one point of entry, which meant that there would be much to secure before repeat visits could be prevented.

It was two days later, towards the end of a dull, wet Saturday afternoon that he became aware of a disturbance in the garden. He was sitting in the kitchen, or rather the scullery section, the place where he gravitated to read the paper or to listen to the radio. It was the lightest space in the house. He heard raised voices and a confrontation, though it was difficult to identify how many intruders there were. After a few moments' indecision Holland quietly lifted the latch on the back door and stepped outside. There were sounds of running and the trampling of vegetation towards the bottom of the garden. Two routes led from the tiled yard area through the garden to the rear of the property. Holland thought of them as the main walkway and the secret path. In fact, both were overgrown, moss-covered tracks with obstacles where a tree branch had fallen or a shrub had invaded and enclosed the route. Somewhere in the middle, between the paths, was a lawn – or what had once been a lawn, now with high unmown grass and encroaching brambles.

Holland chose to follow the secret path, telling himself he would have the benefit of coming on the intruders with an element of surprise. It also made him feel more comfortable. There was dampness in the air as well as in the vegetation from the recent rain, so that his trousers and jumper were soon wet as he negotiated the wild walkway that ran partly along the right-hand border of the plot. As the path cut inside towards the area where he had found the shed, Holland heard rustling and whispers to his right, coming from the middle of a dense group of high, wild ferns. These were overlooked by wayward assorted shrubs, small trees and three or four spindly Douglas pines which, with trailing boughs, marked that side of the property. He heard matches being struck and laughter and could smell the sulphur in the damp air.

On the spur of the moment he waded into the undergrowth, sodden from the rainstorm. It was like plunging through a tropical jungle.

Suddenly there seemed to be people running all around him, crashing through the surrounding ferns. Where they flattened out, battered and broken, he could still smell smoke in the air, and there were dead matches, pieces of ripped cigarette packets and cigarette papers strewn on the wet green carpet. To his astonishment there was also a rusted metal stanchion, tall and imposing, supported by machinery at the base, and topped by a still-intact, downward-pointing red railway signal.

Holland gasped. The signal had been hidden from the path by the fronds of the Douglas pines, masked by a feathery greenery that might have left it undiscovered for years. What else might lie undiscovered in this extraordinary, wild garden? He bent down and picked up an abandoned lighter.

Just as Holland registered it was quiet around him, so the disturbance recommenced. It was close to him. There was a rampaging like a whirlwind and the sound of trampling on vegetation. He pursued the sound, finding a track of broken, beaten tendrils and damaged bushes.

As he came out onto the main path, he caught a glimpse of someone ahead of him, one of the children, and then there was a crash, groan and silence. Tentatively Holland made his way along and stopped when he saw a figure flat on the ground. The child that he had been pursuing turned and looked up at him, pulling himself up. It was a young lad rather than a child, small and stocky, grimacing from pain.

'You're trespassing,' said Holland, not sure what he should say or do now that he could confront one of the intruders. Inside he was still aglow with the find of the railway signal.

'You made me fall,' said the lad, trying to get up.

Holland stood still, concerned. He remembered his father's reaction when he had caught the young offenders on his property, the beating that had been administered, and he shuddered.

'Are you alright?' he asked.

'I've hurt my ankle,' the boy replied. 'I can't walk.'

'I'd better help you,' said Holland. He gingerly put his hand under the boy's arm and started to help him up. Horrified, he realised that he was going to have to do something. 'How old are you?' he asked. 'Do you live near here?'

'Thirteen.' He didn't respond as to where he lived.

'We'd better get you down to the house,' said Holland.

The boy put his arm round Holland's shoulder and leaned his weight on him as they hobbled down the path towards the kitchen door.

'Where are your friends?' asked Holland. 'There were more of you.'

'They've gone.'

Inside the scullery Holland sat the youth down at the kitchen table.

'Perhaps you'll be able to walk in a minute or two when you've rested it.'

'Maybe,' he replied.

'Do you want a drink? I've got some orange juice.' Holland went back through and searched his kitchen cupboards for the bottle of orange squash he vaguely remembered purchasing. He was aware of the lad watching him, following his movements.

'Where did you get that clock from?' the boy asked suddenly, looking at the railway clock which still sat in the middle of the table like an icon.

'It belonged to my family,' said Holland quickly.

'Like an heirloom?'

Holland held out the glass of squash and it was drained in a single swig.

'Your garden's very overgrown. I do gardening work if you need some help.'

The idea of recruiting help, in this way, had not occurred to Holland before. He was excited by the prospect.

'You mean at weekends?' he said.

'Anytime,' said the boy.

'What about school?'

'Evenings and weekends. Interested?'

'Yes,' said Holland.

The boy stood up and carefully tested his foot against the ground.

'I'll be able to get on my way now.'

'Are you sure?' said Holland, considerably relieved.

'You won't have any more trouble in the garden. Not if I'm working here.'

Holland smiled. 'Thank you,' he said.

'I'll come back and see you. Sort it out.' They went outside.

The boy turned when they reached the back gate. 'Have you got my lighter?' he asked. Holland did not respond and the lad shrugged.

After he'd gone Holland went back up the secret path to look at his new-found signal. He could not believe his luck.

3

On the following Monday morning Holland was enjoying a late breakfast, having finally mastered the art of boiling eggs the way his mother had done them. He was only halfway through eating when the doorbell rang. He paused.

This was the first time since Holland had moved in that he recalled the doorbell ringing. He knew the sound because he had experimented with the bell to find out whether it worked, and to see where it could be heard in the house. It was in the kitchen and scullery where the sound was loudest. He thought this might be a throwback to the days of servants. The house was probably big enough for there to have been a maid, or maybe two, and the kitchen was inevitably where they would have spent most of their day.

Holland wondered if it was the boy, come back to discuss the gardening work. Reluctantly he decided to answer. He didn't want to lose the opportunity to obtain help when it had been offered in this way, and he had no way of contacting the lad himself; he didn't even know his name. Before he went to the door he cleared his plate from the table, and as an afterthought carefully placed the railway clock in a drawer in the dresser.

Holland could see an outline of someone through the frosted glass of the front door. It certainly wasn't the boy. However, the person would also be aware of him, and it was too late to withdraw and not answer. He undid the top and bottom bolts and turned the deadlock key, a key that was permanently stuck in the inside of the door lock. His visitor was a woman. She looked nervous, but she had an open, friendly smile. Holland was not good at estimating age but he guessed she was somewhere in her later forties, certainly not young, but young compared to him.

'Good morning,' she said, quietly. 'I wrote to you… I used to live here.'

Holland had assumed the writer of the letter on pale blue paper to be male.

'I wondered if it would be possible to have a look round the house, if it's not putting you out… this house belonged to my family for many years.' He noticed that she was trembling with emotion.

Holland recognised his own reluctance to engage, but was also torn between that and a curiosity to find out about the history of his house, and especially the history of the railway memorabilia that he was uncovering in the garden.

'Would you like to come in?' he said. 'I was just about to make some coffee.'

They went through into the scullery, Holland aware that though he was leading the way the layout would clearly be familiar to his guest.

In the scullery the woman immediately sat at the table. 'It's not changed,' she said.

Holland went into the kitchen, filled the kettle and then came back and watched the woman as her eyes flickered around the room. She got up and moved to the window to look out into the yard and the small, empty outbuildings that enclosed it from the other side. There was a part-view of the garden and she gave a little gasp.

'The garden has become very overgrown,' she said.

'I've not been here very long,' he said, by way of justification. 'There's a lot to do, I know.' He was vaguely aware that she didn't have a handbag with her, which to him seemed slightly odd.

He filled the coffee pot, judging that ground coffee was appropriate on this occasion, rather than instant. He also brought his mother's china coffee cups, milk jug and sugar bowl through to the table.

'How long ago did you live here?' he asked at last.

'I left in 1980,' she said. 'Then my father lived here by himself.'

'So, you were a child here…?'

'My family owned the house from when it was built.'

Holland was disconcerted. Why had the house remained empty and apparently abandoned for over twenty years prior to his purchase?

'Have you been away?'

'Yes,' she said.

'Abroad?'

'Canada.' She was clearly restless, anxious to see the remainder of the property. He wasn't sure whether he should accompany her or not, but on the whole felt that it was reasonable he went with her. She was, after all, a stranger to him.

'I'm glad to see it now,' she said, as they went upstairs. 'Before you make any changes.' She paused on the landing. 'That was my room,' she said, pointing to the back bedroom that lay above the scullery and kitchen.

'Do go in,' he offered.

The back bedroom was sparsely furnished. Holland had spread the accumulated belongings of his own family over the three bedrooms and box room of which he now had possession. She sat down on the bed and looked wonderingly around the room.

'Perhaps I should leave you for a bit,' he said.

'That would be very kind.'

A little later she reappeared in the scullery.

'Your coffee has gone cold,' he said.

'Never mind,' she replied. 'Would it be alright to have a walk round the garden?'

'I'm afraid it is very overgrown. As I said I've not yet had time to clear it up. I have got plans, though,' he added.

'So all the railway things are still there?'

'Yes! I'd be interested to know where they came from. I'm an enthusiast myself.'

'Really?' she said. 'I used to love playing with them when I was a child. They were all put in place before the war. My grandfather worked for the Great Western Railway.'

Holland positively beamed. 'I worked for the railways myself. In fact, it was seeing the railway memorabilia that convinced me to buy the house. I'd like to know more about it – if you know anything, that is?'

'I have some pictures you might like to see,' she responded. 'Of the garden in the 1930s. It almost looks like railway property! If it's not an imposition I could come back another time and bring them to show you.'

'Thank you very much,' he said.

Whilst she was in the garden he fretted about the children and hoped that she wouldn't be disturbed by the uninvited visitors as he had been himself. On the other hand, the boy had seemed certain he could stop them coming back. As it happened she was not outside for very long and when she came back she looked disappointed.

'It is terribly overgrown. I wasn't really able to get round very much of it. I couldn't find the lawn.'

'I've got great plans though,' he said. 'It will be very helpful to see the old photographs.'

They arranged she would return the following week, though she couldn't confirm on which day.

4

After the woman left Holland experienced a spectrum of emotions. On the one hand he was thrilled to think he would have a chance to see pictures of the railway memorabilia as it had once been, providing a blueprint for how he might restore it. On the other he was deeply troubled and anxious about the railway clock. He felt the woman's relationship to the house, and its past, somehow gave her a right over it. He dreaded her opening the dresser drawer and pulling out the clock, perhaps reclaiming it, as well as the other memorabilia dotted around the garden. Of course he knew he had bought the contents of both house and garden when he purchased the house, but there was something emotionally and morally about his visitor's rights that left him doubtful, as if he was an invader.

He wondered how it was that she had left the place to deteriorate, to the point where it had been abandoned. Was she aware of what had happened? Had she been abroad all that time? What had become of her father? He liked the woman but these questions left him feeling very uneasy.

Despite this agitation, Holland felt a purpose that he had not experienced before. Passing a neighbour in the street he spoke for the first time, exchanging pleasantries, and then thought afterwards that the neighbours might be a further source of useful information about the history of his property. Perhaps one of them might even have been there when the woman was living at home. That was another mini-project to be undertaken in the not-too-distant future.

And then the boy came back.

He appeared at the back kitchen door one morning, and before Holland had time to get up and answer the knock, the lad was peering through the window at him sitting at the scullery table. He got up slowly and went to the door.

'I've come to do the garden. Like you said.'

'Now?' asked Holland. 'What about school?'

'It's a holiday today,' he replied. He appeared to be walking without any difficulty.

'You'd better come in,' said Holland, not quite knowing what to say next. But the boy did the running for him, naming an hourly rate, saying he'd be paid each time he came and that he'd need to come into the kitchen to get drinks from time to time. It all seemed quite easy, and Holland relaxed.

'Where do you want me to start?'

Suddenly the magnitude of the task confronted Holland once more.

'Do you want me to clear the lawn?'

'No,' Holland decided. 'The signal – make a clear way through to the signal. That's the first thing, yes.'

'Alright. And you don't want the others coming back, do you?'

'I'd like to stop them.'

'Don't worry, I told you I'll stop them,' said the boy.

'It's not just that,' said Holland. 'At least, it would be good to stop the… intruders.'

'Intruders?' The lad laughed. 'It's just kids.'

'We'll also need to find out where they get in. Still, you probably know that.'

'You mean put up security?'

'I'm not sure what's needed,' said Holland. 'Perhaps we should have a look.'

'I shall keep watch. So why do you want me to do the signal?'

'I want to see if it works.'

'Alright.' He didn't question why this was important. 'I'll need some tools.'

'There are some in the shed. I'll show you.'

They spent the next hour or so in the garden, firstly looking at the collection of old tools and implements, some of which Holland had brought with him and some of which had been left with the house. Then the boy showed him some of the ways he and others came into the space. It was clear the entry points would take some considerable work to seal. There were routes beneath and through hedges and across broken fences. There was right of way access behind the plot, which made it easier to get into Holland's property, though there were also entrances through adjoining gardens as well.

'You've got the biggest garden,' said the boy, 'by far.'

Holland lingered by the platform bench and Great Western Railway gate. He found that the gate was off its hinge at the top and wouldn't swing open as it should. It was perfectly easy to walk round it, but that wasn't the point.

'You like this old railway stuff, don't you. Is that why you want me to clear the signal?'

'Yes, it was hidden before. I didn't know it was there,' said Holland.

The lad looked at him curiously. 'Well, I'd better get on then,' he said.

Back in the house Holland went into the dining-room, overlooking the back yard, a room which he rarely used but where he had set up his computer. For the first time in several days he sat down and started to undertake some railway research. He was particularly interested to uncover the history of the Great Western Railway viaduct which had apparently been demolished in 1889.

He wondered what role the woman's grandfather had played in the GWR and whether the clock had been presented to him as a gift or memento. Holland became absorbed in his task and time slipped.

He looked up to see the boy standing outside in the yard, watching him through the window.

Holland got up and went out. 'Would you like a drink?' he said.

They sat in the scullery together whilst the boy drank orange juice and ate half a packet of biscuits.

'I don't know your name,' he said.

'John. What's yours?'

'Mr Holland. You can call me Holland.'

'Holland? What's happened to that clock?' he said suddenly. 'You had it on the table when I was here before.'

'It's gone to be repaired,' said Holland. 'Do you live near here?'

'Not far,' the lad replied. 'Come and see what I've done.'

At the far end of the secret path there was now a cleared way through the ferns and undergrowth to the signal. It was wide enough to comfortably walk through without getting drenched from the vegetation on either side when it was wet. The boy had cut some of the lower boughs of the nearest pine, so that more of the signal stanchion was visible from a distance, but a ladder would be needed to climb up and remove enough to fully open the signal to view. He'd also cleared the ground around it. Together they inspected the base and mechanism.

'It's all rusted,' said the boy.

'It's seized up,' said Holland. 'It's not going to be easy to unlock.' He was disappointed, though he hadn't really expected that they would make it operable in one day. The signal remained pointing down to the ground at a forty-five degree angle. Still, Holland brightened at the prospect of what else could be achieved now that he had help.

'Is that shed from the railway too?' his companion asked.

'It's an old ticket office, from a small, sideline station, late nineteenth century I would say.' Holland replied.

'You know lots don't you. Shall I clear that out next?'

'That would be very good.'

Holland was surprised at the amount John achieved on that first day. A pile of old tins, flower pots, rusted tools and garden boxes accumulated outside the ticket office as gradually more of the interior was accessed. Holland realised he would need additional means to dispose of both the garden waste and other rubbish that was one outcome of the work. It was too much to put out with the normal refuse bins.

'We could have a fire,' said the boy.

Holland was not sure about that. 'In any case we can't burn tins.'

'I could dig a hole. Bury them,'

'That's a lot of work,' said Holland.

'That's alright. As long as you can afford the time,' he replied.

Later, as Holland sat once again at his computer, he became aware of the boy urgently signalling from outside the window. As he had explored further into the old ticket office he had found loose and boxed papers that had come with the building – there were duplicate, template forms to record freight movements, parcel arrivals and ticket sales. The find brought the ticket office to life, though Holland was aware that there was nothing of special interest or value. It was John's turn to be disappointed, so Holland shared his museum idea and vision.

'Well, if you go ahead you could always sell these as souvenirs,' the boy said.

Holland was touched by the way his museum concept had inspired his new friend.

'You should have some of these,' he said. 'As extra payment for your work.'

'Thanks,' he said, and went off quite jauntily with a batch of ticket office forms and a few pounds in his pocket. He insisted he would come back the next day and did, bringing a new can of oil to have a go at freeing the signal mechanism. Holland offered him money for the oil but he said he didn't need it. They worked together for a while, with cloths and oil, before acknowledging that it was going to take more robust methods to release the signal from its years of rusted neglect.

Meeting his immediate neighbour again, Holland had a longer conversation in which proper introductions were made. The neighbour was curious about the visits he was getting from the lad. 'Do you mind?' she said.

Holland revealed the help that he was getting in the garden and his plans for renovation, though he didn't go so far as to share the concept of the railway museum. The woman was pleasant and friendly, though she also seemed puzzled by what he was doing.

'The place has been neglected for so long,' she said. 'Empty since I've been here, until you came along. There must be lots you need to do in the house itself, never mind outside.'

He asked whether any of the other neighbours had been there long enough to remember the former occupants.

'You could speak to Mrs Bartlett,' she said. 'She's been here for years.'

For much of that week the lad came back each day, never at the same time, but always able to put in at least a few hours' work. He even dug the promised hole, though a little shallow in Holland's view, to bury some of the rubbish from the old ticket office.

Holland started to worry about the boy's school, and how much his parents knew about what he was doing, but John shrugged off questions and seemed unconcerned about any implications of the time he was spending in the garden.

Talking more to the boy about his museum scheme made it seem real and achievable. Holland dug out an old album of railway engine postcards that he treasured and showed it off, explaining the different classes of steam locomotive and the range of companies and operations that existed before nationalisation. However, Holland realised that they were spending more time in the dining room, looking at his research and his personal collection of railway memorabilia, and less time actually clearing the garden itself. He also became aware that the boy's hours of work seemed to decrease on a daily basis.

But, for the first time in his life Holland was opening up, like a rarely blooming flower.

5

On the day the woman returned, later the following week, John was already there. Holland had asked him to clear moss and dirt off the platform bench, ready to sand it down and apply a coat of preservative. Holland sensed some resistance to the task. He wasn't sure why. However, he had been pleasantly surprised not to receive any other visitors in the garden the weekend before. It seemed as if the boy might have the influence that he had intimated. The railway clock remained in the scullery drawer where it had lain untouched for over a week.

Immediately the doorbell rang he knew that it would be her. He was sitting at his computer in the dining room contemplating plans for a route around the museum garden. It was coming increasingly alive in his head and involved the construction of a high wall all the way round to prevent unwanted access. He persuaded himself the wall was about controlling access to the museum; in reality he wanted to keep people out. In Holland's vision he wandered about the completed project, satisfied with the content and the layout, but in his imagination there were never any visitors.

He went into the hallway and through the ritual of unbolting and unlocking the door.

'I've come back,' she said. 'I thought you'd like to see those pictures.' She was carrying a folder. This time she came more confidently into the house and it seemed natural to lead her into the dining room.

By the time he had made some coffee and brought it through the woman had spread her pictures out on the dining room table. They were black and white, some quite small and a little faded. The location of a number of the views in the garden would not have been recognisable were it not for the positioning of the railway items.

The signal stood tall and clear, its arm at right angles to the stanchion. The trees were mere saplings at the side. In several pictures there were people: an elderly man in an Edwardian suit and tie; a young girl; an older boy, rakish-looking with cap askew and a confident smile, perhaps about the age of the boy who was even now working in the garden.

But the picture that immediately leapt out was an interior shot without any people. He was sure, based on the location of the window, that it was taken in the dining room where they were now sitting. The room was full of furniture, and sitting on the mantelpiece, along with other decorative and functional items, was the railway clock. He blushed and felt immediate apprehension but the woman did not appear to register anything.

'You said it was your grandfather who installed the railway memorabilia?' he said.

'Anything that was going to be replaced by the railway he brought here,' she said. 'I remember the signal was a particular challenge. It was brought on a horse and cart!'

'But surely there were vehicles, I thought you said it was put in just before the war?'

'Yes, it was, so I believe,' the woman responded quickly. 'My grandfather told me the story. My father helped with everything and then maintained the garden and the railway trail after grandfather died.'

'The trail?' asked Holland.

'The paths around the garden were laid out so that you could explore all the different railway objects, but the lawn was kept separate in the middle, as a kind of sanctuary. It was to please my grandmother. You couldn't see any railway objects from there.'

'Can you remember the layout of the paths for the trail?' asked Holland.

'Yes, of course, I explored them so often as a child. It was quite magical,' she said. 'Occasionally other children used to come and play with us too, my brother and I, but grandfather didn't want too many people to know about it.'

'I told you I had plans,' said Holland. He went on with a rush of enthusiasm, 'I'd like to restore the garden as a kind of railway museum.'

'You mean for people to come to?'

'Yes,' said Holland, a little hesitantly.

'That would be very fitting. My father was solitary and didn't welcome visitors. I always thought it was a pity the garden wasn't shared. I looked after him for a long time after he was left alone.'

'I looked after my mother too, until she died,' said Holland. He had not spoken with anyone about his mother since he had moved to the house.

'You understand then,' replied the woman.

'And what about your brother – you mentioned a brother?' He felt this might be a route to carefully finding out why the house had been left to dereliction for so long.

'My brother was not able to help. He went away when he was quite young.' She looked sad and Holland felt that he could not press the point.

They sat silent for a few moments and Holland pretended to study the pictures, but he found it hard to focus without coming back to the image that clearly showed the railway clock sitting on the mantelpiece in that very room. He looked up and the woman was absorbed in the space, registering it as if taking photographs in her mind so that she could recall in the future.

'I remember this room so well,' she said, 'as it was.'

'Do you think we could piece together the trail you mentioned through the photographs?' asked Holland. 'Perhaps identify the pathways.'

'I'm afraid I can't leave the photographs with you,' the woman said suddenly.

'Don't worry, I didn't expect that. But it would be helpful to understand how everything links together. The photographs help. Is that your grandfather?' he asked, pointing to the elderly man looking suspiciously at the camera from under his hat.

'Yes.'

'And who are the children?' he asked tentatively.

'The boy is my brother,' she said finally, 'with a friend.'

'He's much older than you?' Holland asked.

'He was. I told you, he went away.'

'When he was young?'

She paused. 'There was a terrible argument with my father. My brother left… he didn't come back. He was a wonderful boy, very adventurous, much too adventurous. He got into trouble… actually, we never saw him again after he left.'

Holland did not know what to say. There was clearly enormous sorrow underlying the lives of the ordinary family who had owned and lived in this house. He felt as if that sorrow must be what accounted for the property being empty and abandoned for such a long period, and perhaps for the decision the woman made to live abroad, in Canada.

Holland looked up at the window to see the boy with his face pressed against it, peering in. Holland felt annoyed that he hadn't knocked at the glass, or even at the back door. He beckoned him to come inside.

'I've got some help with clearing the garden,' he said to the woman. 'It's a local lad called John. He comes in most days,' he added, aware as he spoke that this didn't seem quite right given the boy's age. He found it hard to say the name, "John". It didn't sound real somehow. Holland always thought of him as the boy. Then he realised that perhaps seeing John would bring back sad memories for the woman of her brother, who looked a similar age in the photographs on the table. So he got up and left the dining room to speak with him in the scullery.

'Is everything alright?' he asked.

'I've washed the bench down. I'll have a break while it dries. Can I come in?'

'I've got a visitor at the moment,' said Holland. 'I'll let you know when she's gone.'

John looked at him with an odd expression. 'Did you get any visitors at the weekend? I mean kids coming into the garden,' he added.

'No,' replied Holland. 'It was very quiet.'

'I told you… just how you like it.'

'I suppose so, yes.' He turned and went back into the hall. He was about to go into the dining room but stopped because he could see his visitor was halfway up the stairs. He glanced back behind him at the boy, who was still standing in the scullery watching him, and then he followed the woman upstairs.

He caught up with her on the landing. She was looking round as if searching for something.

'Are you alright?' he asked.

'I'm sorry,' she said. 'There are just so many memories.' She looked on the verge of tears.

'Is it your brother?'

She didn't reply.

'I imagine you were in Canada for many years,' Holland went on.

'Yes. It's all very strange.' And then suddenly she said, 'I think I have to go.'

At the front door she turned back, her folder of photographs under her arm. 'Thank you so much. I do hope you can make the museum happen.'

'Will I not see you again?' he asked. This all seemed to be happening too quickly.

'Maybe.' She walked quickly out of the door and at the gate turned briefly to give a final wave.

'I don't even know your name,' he called after her. But she was gone.

He stood at the door for some moments, then he closed the heavy front door but didn't lock it. He turned round and walked back into the dining room. He felt disconcerted and sat down for a few moments to think.

A noise from the kitchen disturbed him from his reverie.

When he opened the scullery door (which he didn't remember closing) the boy was standing by the dresser. The top drawer was open and John had the railway clock in his hands. He turned and looked at Holland with a knowing expression on his face. He looked older than his years. They stood looking at each other in silence and Holland felt strangely as if he should not step inside the threshold of his own room.

The lad spoke first. 'I thought you said it had been sent away.'

'What are you doing?' Holland said eventually. He was vibrating with anger.

'I was looking for my lighter. You never gave it back.'

'Put that down!'

John did not respond.

'I said put it down, it doesn't belong to you!' Holland moved quickly now, fearful for the clock, though he wasn't sure why. He could feel the blood rising in his face and he felt as if his head and neck were shaking from side to side.

'Alright,' said the boy.

Holland wanted to grip him, shake him, push him against the wall, punish him for invading his space, and for his slyness in finding Holland out. But something inside would not let him touch the boy, at least not while he still held the precious clock. He took his breakfast cup and saucer from the kitchen table, and was aware of the curious rattling caused by his shaking hands, then he threw them down on to the stone floor with a violence that surprised himself. The china shattered into myriad shards. The spasm completed, he sobbed and sank down into his chair. He could not look at John, who placed the clock roughly on the table where it fell on its side.

'I only wanted my lighter,' he said.

Holland did not respond. The shaking was gentler now, like an aftershock. He gripped the chenille cloth, strangely comforted by the feel of the velvety fabric between his fingers and the contrast with the roughness of the tassels that hung round the edges. He would have liked to throw the cloth over the boy to hide him, to make him disappear like a magic trick. Instead, John was still there, standing in front of him, expecting some further reaction.

'So, who was your visitor?' he said at last. Holland detected an attack within the question but did not understand why.

'You'd better go,' he said.

Without a further word the boy turned round and walked out of the back door, back into the garden. He left the door swinging open.

Holland reached over and sat the railway clock back upright. He ran his hands along the smooth polished oak and then traced the raised edge of the circular glass face. The roughness of the gilt at the edge of the glass tuned with the feel of the tassels on his tablecloth.

After a while Holland got up and fetched a soft broom to sweep up the remains of the china cup and saucer. Splinters of china had reached every corner of the room and some had even spilled out into the hallway beyond. Then he went out into the backyard. There was an odd sound coming from the garden, like an animal in the undergrowth snorting or rustling through dead leaves. He followed the main path towards the sound.

When Holland identified the noise, he realised it was John. The boy was bent over, vigorously sanding down the platform bench, working harder than Holland had ever seen him before. Apparently he was unaware of Holland watching him and continued, making strong strokes with the old pieces of sandpaper wrapped round a block of wood that they had salvaged from the ticket office shed. Holland could see that the sanding was a huge job.

John stopped and straightened up. He turned and looked at Holland. He did not seem surprised to see he was being watched, and he smiled as if nothing had happened between them. It was an intimate, warm smile and Holland relaxed.

'I'm getting splinters in my hand,' he said.

'Be careful,' replied Holland. Then he added, 'I'll make a drink, when you're ready.'

The sounds of sanding followed Holland back to the house. He shut the back door. Then he went back through to the dining room and opened the bureau in which he kept official papers. John's lighter was nestled in a pigeonhole along with miscellaneous keys and a collection of railway badges. When he removed the lighter he carefully locked the bureau and pocketed the key.

He squeezed the trigger of the lighter and it burst into life, producing a dangerously high flame and a strong smell of lighter fuel.

Holland stood by the window and watched the boy emerge from the secret path and head into the outdoor toilet. Glancing over at the hearth he had a strong image again of the photograph of the room and of the railway clock with pride of place on the mantelpiece.

Back in the kitchen he prepared drinks and put out the biscuits he knew John liked. The boy knocked before coming in.

'Your visitor's gone then?' he said.

Once again Holland detected a strange element of challenge in the question. However, in his need to register an apology for his earlier behaviour, he shared something of the background to his visitor and the information the woman had brought about the history of the garden.

John listened but offered no comment. Afterwards he simply said once again, 'So, what about my lighter?'

'You need to be careful with this. The flame is very high. Why do you need one anyway?'

The boy held out his hand for the lighter and flinched as his fingers stretched. 'Splinters,' he said. 'Look.' He stood and came over to where Holland was sitting. 'Look.' This time he held out his left hand.

Holland became aware of the smell of the boy. It was not something he had noticed before. Maybe he'd never been this close to him. It was an unwashed smell, not just the sweat from recent hard work. The boy's sleeve was rolled up from the hand he offered out and Holland could see faded scratches and cuts around the arm.

'You need to take more care of yourself,' he said.

The boy stayed completely still for a moment and then said, quietly and authoritatively, 'You can have me if you want me.'

Holland looked up at John's face and the boy placed his right hand on Holland's shoulder. Instinctively Holland pulled away. The boy went back to his seat, and calmly carried on eating biscuits.

'Go now,' said Holland. John stopped eating and looked at him in surprise. Holland did not look at him. 'Go now. Don't come back again. This is finished. Don't come back ever again.'

The boy stood up and looked at Holland. He glanced over at the railway clock and for a moment Holland was afraid he was going to take the clock and smash it to the floor. Then he walked out of the scullery, through the hallway and down the hall. Holland watched him from the scullery door. At the front door he paused and looked back. Then he opened it, went out and slammed it shut behind him.

6

The next two days passed by as if they did not exist. Holland felt paralysed, incapable even of the necessary thinking to make sense of what had happened. He sat around the scullery listlessly and did not want to go into the dining room, or even to open the drawer to look at the railway clock which he'd once again hidden from view, wrapped in a cloth for additional protection. He was not aware of any disturbance in the garden and so assumed the visitors had not returned, but he felt an alienation from the space outside, as if it was not within safe limits for him to wander.

The ringing of the doorbell jolted his recollection that he had not bolted and deadlocked the front door. The persistence of the ringing forced him to go to it, and he could see from the silhouette that it was certainly not John.

Holland could tell from the expression on his neighbour's face that something was wrong. He was also more abrupt himself and looked pale and drawn from lack of proper sustenance over the last two days.

His neighbour was kind but firm. She felt it appropriate to warn Holland that the lad may not be all he appeared, and that she had seen him dispose of rubbish in her hedge following one visit to the house. She produced the bundle of ticket office forms and receipts that Holland had given to John as a gesture of their railway comradeship. He had clearly stuffed them in the hedge on his way home the same day.

After she'd gone Holland locked the door. Something made him go into the dining room and open the cupboard where he stored his railway material and publication collection. The railway album had gone. He was aware of a pounding heart and desperate sense of anguish as he went through the house looking for other places he may have left it. Really, he knew that he wouldn't find it. He last remembered sitting in the dining room with the boy, sharing the images and his own memories, particularly focusing on the picture of the Flying Scotsman and even cautiously revealing the origins of the railway clock as oak from the Great Western Railway viaduct where the Scotsman had run.

In the scullery the clock was still intact, wrapped as he had hidden it in the dresser drawer.

Holland felt uncertain about his position if he called in the police. He didn't know where John lived, nor did he know his surname, and in any case he accepted that he had voluntarily allowed the boy into his house. So, when the police called to see him, at first it seemed meant, rather like the woman arriving to tell him about the history of the house.

Holland took the policemen through to the dining room. They were quiet and courteous, though declining his coffee and preferring to sit on upright chairs rather than the more comfortable sofa that allowed a view through the window. Holland sat on his computer seat.

'You may be wondering why we're here,' began the more senior officer. The other was taking notes.

'Is it about the boy?'

'Which boy are you referring to?'

'Well, there's only really one,' said Holland. 'John is who I meant. I know he has friends that have been in the garden but I've not seen any of them.'

'How long have you known him?' they asked.

Holland felt encouraged by the quiet civility, and shared the whole story of his encounter with John and their subsequent relationship, though he omitted any details of the argument at the end. He concluded by saying he had not seen the boy for several days and that he very much feared that he had taken an item belonging to him.

The officer was interested to know exactly what was missing, how he had become aware of the theft and whether Holland had confronted John and accused him. Holland was reassuring on that point.

'So as far as you're concerned this friend of yours has simply not come back?'

'That's right,' said Holland. 'I'm glad you came because I wasn't really sure what to do.'

There was an uncomfortable silence. At last the policeman spoke.

'Were you expecting us?'

'No. Not at all…' Holland faltered as he replied.

'Didn't it occur to you to find out more about this lad, John, as you were employing him and he's a minor?' the policeman asked.

'It was all very informal. And… it just happened. We were getting to know each other as we went along.'

'You live here alone, do you?'

Holland explained his circumstances and expanded on his purchase of the house.

'And you wanted this boy, John, to help you clear the garden. You didn't think about employing professional help for that?'

'I hadn't considered it… I didn't think I could afford it.'

'You didn't look into it?'

'No.'

The other policeman spoke now, and asked Holland to again take them through everything that had happened in relation to John since the afternoon he'd first met him. Holland particularly focused on how he'd shared his interest in railways and railway memorabilia and how they'd sat together in the dining room looking at his precious album.

'How valuable is the album?' they asked.

'I was once offered £1,500 for the collection. By a railway enthusiast I met at a show. I'd taken the album to share with people there. I was surprised, but I wouldn't sell it.'

'Is it specified in your house insurance?'

'No,' he replied. 'It didn't occur to me anyone would understand its value.'

'Did you tell John how much it was worth?'

'No. I don't think so. He would have seen it meant a lot to me.'

The first policeman stood. 'That's all we need to know for now. However, we will be back to ask you more. Are you at home over the next few days?'

Holland replied that he did not expect to go anywhere.

'Is that your computer?' asked the second policeman as they were leaving the room.

Holland laughed. 'It's new, and I'm just getting used to it,' he said.

'Thank you,' they both said as they left. 'You've been very helpful.'

The knowledge that his theft had been reported took some weight from Holland's mind. He still felt unable to lift the latch of the back door and venture into the garden, but he did continue his research into the GWR viaduct and the source of the oak for the railway clock. He took the clock from the drawer, unwrapped it, and brought it into the dining room as a kind of talisman, placing it on the mantelpiece where it had once stood all those years ago. It seemed poignant that this object, created from materials that had survived a demolition, should be the remaining essence of a family that had lived and died in the house. However, despite following a number of different leads, the viaduct trail ran cold. He could find references to its existence, and to a stone construction that seemed to replace it, but he was disappointed not to find any pictures, or anything that could confirm the date of demolition.

Thinking about pictures from the past made him wonder

whether there was any means to get in touch with the woman who had visited. He considered approaching the older neighbour, Mrs Bartlett, who might remember the family that had lived in the house, and perhaps even the woman herself as a child or young woman.

He opened the bureau to examine the original letter, to see if he could interpret the signature and make out a name, but he couldn't find it. Holland could still see and smell the pale blue envelope and the short note inside. He could remember the contents almost word for word and recreate in his imagination the unreadable signature, but the letter itself was not to be found. He wondered if he had inadvertently slipped it inside the railway album and if it, too, had gone with John.

On the next visit the police officers' demeanour was brusquer; they seemed sharper, and quicker to fire questions. Once more they sat in the dining room and once again refused any refreshments. They wanted to know whether he'd had any other visitors to the house and whether anyone had seen him with the boy. Holland brightened in sharing the visits from the woman, though he felt embarrassed about not knowing her name. He explained how her letter had arrived, closely followed by the woman herself, and that John had been there during one of her visits.

They asked to see the letter and Holland revealed he thought it had been taken along with the railway album. They were persistent in asking Holland whether John had seen him and his visitor to-gether, and Holland described looking up to find the boy watching them through the window.

'He was spying on you?' they asked.

'I wouldn't have put it like that,' responded Holland. He was starting to feel very anxious. His unease increased when one of the officers stood and went over to the railway clock.

'This looks very old. I don't think it was here last time we came.'

'No,' said Holland. 'It was in a drawer.' He felt it was wise not to make up a story for the police, even at the risk of jeopardising his ownership of the clock. So, he told them how he had found it and about putting it away when his visitor had called, though he didn't mention the picture which showed the clock in its rightful place on the mantelpiece. On a sudden impulse he shared his neighbour's observation that perhaps Mrs Bartlett would remember the people who had lived in the house and even recall a name.

Then they asked him about the other young person, the one who had disappeared. Holland was completely taken aback. He didn't remember telling John about the woman's brother, the one who had "gone away". He must have been listening, either at the window or the door. Surely that was the only way to account for it, unless perhaps he *had* told John. He couldn't be sure. Holland started to feel very muddled about what the woman had told him, what he had inferred from the photographs she brought, what he had or hadn't told John, and what the boy might have gleaned from eavesdropping. The policemen were pushing him for information he simply didn't have, and he lost his temper. He screamed at them in a childish tantrum, shouting that he didn't know anything about the child who had disappeared. Then he spluttered to a stop.

When they left this time Holland was sure they were going to say they would take the railway clock with them. Instead, they took his computer.

7

Events then moved rapidly and enveloped Holland as if in a dream. A team arrived and erected various barriers and tents in his garden.

Through his dining room window Holland was able to see that a lot of activity was taking place.

Different policemen came into the house to interview him. Generally, they asked the same questions again and again, though by now he had determined that he needed to tell them everything, including the incident with the clock when he had found the boy rifling the drawer and had smashed the cup and saucer in his anger. At last they revealed their own version of events to him.

They told him that a serious allegation had been made. He had been accused of ill-treating the boy – more, of abusing him. He was accused of sexual activity with a minor. Furthermore, it seemed that John was in care, and lived in a children's home. The various visitors to Holland's garden were other young people from the same home, or connections the children had made with a number of undesirable associates, the garden being used for a range of inappropriate activity. Now Holland felt obliged to share the final incident, the last scene he had had with John, but he could see it was too late. It looked as if he were making it up in response to knowledge of the complaint that had been made. The policeman asked him about the recent digging in the garden and Holland explained that the boy had dug a shallow trench to bury rubbish. With this at least they seemed satisfied. They did not explain why they were also digging in his garden.

Then, suddenly the barriers were removed and the tents were taken away. Holland could see that a considerable amount of clearing work had been undertaken. This was not how he had expected the renovation of the garden museum would take place. They explained they were satisfied.

However, they were clearly not satisfied with his account of the visitor from the past. They seemed to think Holland had been wasting their time, perhaps deliberately.

'There was no visitor,' they said.

John had not seen anyone, either when he looked through the window or when he came into the house, or so he said. Furthermore, investigation had shown that after the elderly man who previously owned the house had died, the property had been left to a distant relative in Canada who had never been traced. That was why the house had been left empty for so long, until the Local Authority was able to take possession and offer it at auction.

They had also talked to Mrs Bartlett. The old man did have two children, a boy and girl. The son was older, a livewire who deeply upset his father with his wayward tendencies. After a final, irrevocable argument, he had left, signed up for active service and had subsequently been killed during the liberation of Florence in August 1944. After he'd left home he had apparently not been mentioned again. Mrs Bartlett said that the family knew he had been killed in Italy, but would not acknowledge his death. It was particularly difficult for the sister, she recalled, who had been inordinately fond of her elder brother. She remained at home, looking after her father, until she too died, aged fifty, in 1980.

8

Holland found himself dreaming, vividly, frequently and sometimes disturbingly, and for the first time that he could recall he woke with detailed memories of his dreams. He started to look forward to going to bed, and to his nocturnal world where anything was possible and where resolution could take place. There was a life in his dreaming.

Often he dreamt about childhood, his own and others', in particular about the girl and boy who had played in the garden of his house back in the 1930s. He saw, as if in a simulation, the garden as it was then, the excitement generated by the arrival of some new pieces of railway memorabilia, and the stirring of the imagination and the sense of adventure of the young boy who first saw a world to explore through "God's Wonderful Railway". In the background was the collector, the grandfather, making sense of his life through his acquisitions and railway creations, finding meaning and purpose and a way to leave his mark on the world. There was also the shadowy figure of the father, scared and limiting, a person closing down opportunity both for himself and for his children.

In his dream Holland hero-worshipped the young boy. He was fearless, courageous and adventurous, a comic-book idol who would always win. He was the boy that Holland wished to have been.

For those growing children the garden was an escape into the world of imagination and travel, as the railway had been for their grandfather. The grandfather was old enough to have experienced the opening of opportunity that came through the development of the rail network. He wanted to celebrate that freedom and passed on his enthusiasm to his grandson. It missed a generation.

The grandson brought friends to the garden and led the imaginative fantasies that developed. They created hideaways, even though the garden was less mature at that time. In due course they took to leaving their own space, sometimes unseen, and to continuing their exploration, both of their imagination and themselves, in the countryside around. As they got older the exploration became more adventurous, more personal and more dangerous. Occasionally the lad allowed his sister to participate. Generally, she was on the fringes, admiring from afar.

Holland started to dream himself into the games, to be one of the boy's team, a participant and adventurer, something he had never been in real life. For the first time he explored his sexuality in these dreams. There was touching and exposure, sharing of private parts, and Holland became aware of what excited him.

Sometimes they would play out events and happenings from

the real world, including resistance to fascism and the Spanish Civil War. The games were helped by first-hand newspaper accounts, collected by the lad and taken into the garden in a precious scrapbook. It comprised a series of leader pages from throughout the early 1930s, the pages kept long after interest in the content had evaporated. The pages were battered and torn as a result of being used as reference in the games.

Holland dreamed one episode in which the lad was much older. In a bedroom in the house the young man was sitting dressed in uniform. He was reviewing the precious scrapbook, but looking back at the leader pages with a sense of detachment. The game had now become real.

On the young man's table, in front of him, was the railway clock. It was placed in the same way that Holland, years later, would place the clock on the kitchen table in the same house, with the same acknowledgement of its value and importance. It was an iconic object and moment. Holland knew instinctively in the dream that the clock had been given to the boy by his grandfather. It had been a parting gift. Now the grandson was also parting, going to war, fulfilling his sense of adventure and his need to make a mark.

On his bed the young man had placed a fresh, pale blue cardboard box. He removed the lid and abruptly started to crumple the leader sheets from his scrapbook one after another, placing them in the box to make a nest. Then he took a piece of thin blue notepaper and wrote a short note to his sister, sealing it in a matching envelope which he placed by the box. He carefully lifted the railway clock and placed it into the nest of papers, then got up and left the room with the box, leaving the envelope and the lid of the box on his table.

It was June 1943, the month that Holland was born.

9

As the weeks passed Holland could see that his garden was be-coming like a bomb site. There were the scars left by the police investigation and then increasingly, from what he could witness from his window, wilful damage inflicted by a constant stream of intruders. He noticed that words had been scrawled on the walls of the outbuildings and outside toilet. A sheet of corrugated asbestos had been pulled off one small roof and flung to the yard. He could see broken tree branches deliberately vandalised. A crack appeared in the glass of the dining room window, presumably from a stone thrown from within the yard itself. He did not go outside.

Meanwhile legal proceedings had moved forward. Holland had been formally charged, allowed bail against the asset of his property and found himself more or less a prisoner in his house. Occasionally he scuttled down the road to catch a bus to visit his solicitor. On these occasions he invariably found himself going into shops where he was not known and could not be recognised, coming back bur-dened down with bags of unnecessary shopping, bought in despera-tion, and much of which he ended up throwing away rather than consuming. Sometimes he saw his neighbour on the other side of the road, always on the other side, and he missed the modest rap-port and communication that had previously taken place.

In addition to the charge of sexually assaulting a minor, Holland was told that the initial investigation had also considered that he might have "done away" with the other child, the one who had pre-viously disappeared. It was only later that it became clear this was a historic story and then that accusation was dropped. From time to time Holland's solicitor came to the house. This was now the only time when the front door bell rang.

Very quickly Holland had come to the conclusion that his solicitor did not believe his version of events. For a start there was the issue of the woman from the past. Holland could not provide any evidence of her existence, nor could he deny her simply because he was advised that this might be in his best interests. It appeared some half-hearted attempt to trace her was undertaken, but Holland knew it was not delivered with any conviction. He was asked lots of questions about his sexual experience which he found extremely difficult to answer. They didn't seem to believe that this was an area of life about which he had always been relatively unconcerned. It was as if not admitting to strong sexual urges was evidence that you were concealing the truth. They even asked him if he'd had fantasies about the woman from the past.

Once the trial commenced, his legal team increasingly warned him that there was a strong chance he would be convicted. It seemed unfathomable to Holland, who was also unable to convince his barrister of the importance of the railway clock, which remained on the dining room mantelpiece, at the periphery of the events unfolding around its owner. In the end they even advised him to change his plea and admit guilt.

The evening before the verdict was due, Holland sat at his kitchen table in the scullery musing over what might happen. He had brought the railway clock through from its place in the dining room and once more placed it in the centre of the table. He looked at it lovingly, then removed the back panel to view the intricacy of the internal mechanism, and to read the inscription on the curling gummed paper. He remembered that he had some glue in a drawer in the kitchen and fetched it in order to secure back the gummed paper.

Clock case made of oak taken from the viaduct of the Great Western Railway, demolished 1889.

Holland wondered about the future. He knew that his dream for the railway museum was no longer to be fulfilled. In fact, he suspected that by the time he returned to the garden he might even find the existing memorabilia had been destroyed or removed. It was ironic that the house was to be potentially subject to a further period of emptiness and dereliction.

He went and fetched the discoloured, cardboard box with its nest of crumpled pages. He lifted the railway clock once again and found that his hands were trembling. He took the clock key and managed to insert it into the winding mechanism once more, despite the uncontrollable shaking of his fingers. Holland wound the clock, rehung the back panel, and then placed the clock back in its cocoon of newspaper in the box. Then he went upstairs, up into the attic and replaced the box where he had found it those many months before.

Holland didn't dream that night.

In the attic the railway clock continued ticking.

It continued ticking for some time, until the mechanism finally wound down.

OBSESSION

Jeremy's Journal

I HAVE SPOKEN WITH AMY.

The opportunity finally came on the crumbling terrace of the ruined Governor's Palace at Uxmal. She was frightened by a red rump tarantula that was basking in the sun!

It is day four of our twelve-day tour of the Yucatan.

Today I have decided to break my lifelong rule and write a journal. It has been a momentous four days that will change the future shape of my life. What a smart decision it was to take early retirement.

I am high and have been floating ever since that magical stop near Xkeken, on day one. The minibus slowed to prevent thousands of yellow butterflies from being pressed flat against the windscreen. We came to a halt and most people got out, some to try and capture the scene on mobile phones, a few, like me, to simply gaze in awe at the sight.

Amy emerged from the swirling butterfly cloud as if she had just materialised in that place, as if she had broken out of a cocoon. It was like a scene in an opera. She was walking towards me as a beautiful spectre. It felt like a moment of destiny. She did not speak.

As we re-boarded the bus, and the butterflies veered away, I scanned the other passengers to make sure Amy really was with us, and had not been transported away in the gigantic, trembling swarm of Mexican Yellows. She was behind me, towards the back of the bus. She was sitting next to another woman, a friend, or maybe her sister. I could sense her presence. Irritatingly, the woman in front of me turned and tried to engage in conversation about the phenomenon we had just seen. This was a sacred moment and I did not want it interrupted. I cut her short and allowed myself to daydream. There was plenty of time to connect with Amy. Twelve days in fact.

At the Cenote Dzitnup, descending the many slippery steps to the water required some care. My enjoyment of the semi-lit interior – the sun was focused through the sink hole like a searchlight to the pristine blue of the water – was jarred by my tour companions. Marjorie, from the seat in front of me, was exposing too much corpulent flesh in a swim costume that left little to the imagination. Half way down the steps she caught up with the elderly couple (who I later discovered were the irascible Clive and his demure wife Jemima) and was enlisted to help them. Progress was slow and I soon reached them. There was little choice but to also offer an arm and support. Clive seemed to think that a lift should be installed. At the bottom he complained that there wasn't a shallow end for ac-climatization. At the pool itself, Marjorie heaved herself in to create an undignified surge across the otherwise tranquil surface. It was an opportunity to practise my clean diving, honed by my period as a diplomat in Oman (water sports were always on the daily sched-ule). I noticed Amy, with her colleague, watching from the viewing gallery. I felt like waving, but that would have been too soon.

She must have been on the bus all the time, since we boarded at Cancun. I had only taken a cursory look at my fellow travellers – it seems that there are fifteen of us – but I was more focused on reading the itinerary and the stories about the Mayan ruins at Chichen Itza, our first scheduled stopover. I had skipped the first group dinner in order to be at the pyramid in time to experience the light show, presenting the descent of Kukulkan, the serpent god. A touch of the Garden of Eden, a day ahead of that vision appearing from the butterfly cloud.

At Izamal I had still not been introduced to the group, who were clearly all getting to know each other. I would reveal my credentials later, hoping to engage with Amy for the first time in a more romantic setting than a hotel restaurant. The yellow town seemed the perfect location, a suitable follow-on to the thrill of the butterflies, and a place that reminded me of Mediterranean towns where I have been posted.

I missed her at the Franciscan convent, the centrepiece of Izamal. I guessed that she and her companion had hired the equivalent of a local taxi to visit the pyramids, one of which is reputedly the second highest in Mexico. My own horse and cart serenaded me around the town, but plodded when I wanted to gallop. My guide did not seem to understand my desire to reach the main monument, insisting, 'You have time.' I could hardly say, 'follow that horse and cart.'

Bizarrely it appears there are remnants of five pyramids in Izamal, most of which are now piles of rubble surrounded by luxuriant vegetation. We caught up with Amy and companion at two monuments before the main event, but each time they were leaving as I clip-clopped to a halt. The second time I raised my hat, but she did not appear to notice. In turn, as I was leaving, Marjorie pulled up behind my conveyance and shouted a boisterous, 'yoohoo', which seemed entirely inappropriate to the location. I pretended not to hear.

Finally, at the great pyramid of Kinich Kak Moo (the sun-eyed fire macaw) I caught up with them. They had reached the summit and were taking in the 360-degree view as I climbed the interminable steps to the top. Amy noticed me and nudged her friend, then they disappeared, stepping further back on the flat platform at the top. My pristine linen suit was dripping with perspiration by the time I reached where they had been standing. Now I saw them disappear down the south side of the monument, though Amy did glance back as they descended. Perhaps it was best to wait for a more opportune moment.

That moment came at Uxmal today. On this occasion we were on foot all the time, so I was able to watch her movements around the ruins and to time my clamber onto the terrace of the Governor's Palace to perfection.

The tarantula had chosen that spot as if by divine providence. Amy was wearing a white, pleated skirt, cut just above the knees, and a short-sleeved blouse which accentuated her breasts. Her legs and arms were gently tanned. She had taken off her sunglasses and her wavy brown hair was billowing in the gentle breeze. She was standing still, frozen as a statue, facing me, as if waiting for me to rescue her. I could see her focus on the spider, her fear.

'Don't be scared,' I said.

'I don't like spiders.'

'Just slowly step over it.'

'It's big… and furry.'

'It won't hurt you.'

'How do you know?'

'It's a red rump tarantula. The bite is virtually harmless. In any case it won't bite you.'

I held out my hands, and nervously she clasped them, closed her eyes and stepped over the spider. I walked backwards, with her still holding both my hands. Then she seemed to realise the contact and in a flush of embarrassment let go.

'Sorry,' she said. 'I don't know what came over me.' There was a pause. 'I don't know where my friend is.'

'I'm glad to have a chance to say hello,' I said. 'Although we have met before.'

'Really'

'Many years ago. It's Jeremy.'

So, I'm up to date. Amy has not changed. I see her as when I first met her, thirty-five years ago. I would have recognised her anywhere. She seemed reluctant to talk about the past. She smiled though when I asked if she was with her sister. 'My friend,' she said.

'I'm travelling alone,' I replied.

We are in Campeche now. This evening I decided to join the group for dinner. We were spread across two tables and it was rather trying to make conversation with the eternal travellers, John and Janice, while my whole attention was focused on Amy at the next table. J and J latched onto my professional career and wanted a detailed breakdown of my CV and the places I have been posted. In each case they had been there and done it, in their attempt to have visited every country in the world. The younger couple, Ryan and Isabelle, were more aloof, though Ryan it seems is a musician and aspiring actor, and was rather impressed that my grandfather was a friend of Edward Elgar. Unfortunately, that also encouraged Marjorie, who it seems sings in a local choir, the highlight for which was a performance of *The Dream of Gerontius.* I wish now I had not mentioned the Elgar connection.

Meanwhile I was in danger of losing the chance to speak further with Amy. I called the waiter, asked him what Amy was drinking, and ordered her another Paloma cocktail. It was fun to see her start of surprise and blush when it arrived by her place. Her friend, I noticed, gave me a quizzical look. I wonder if Amy has spoken of our shared past.

Amy and friend left the table early, though they did stop momentarily and Amy thanked me for the drink and for saving her from the tarantula. Her friend is called Becky. Rather common I thought. The spider story sparked reminiscences from J and J about their experiences in Mexico City, leading to an unnecessarily detailed description of the injuries suffered by Frida Kahlo when she was involved in the famous tram accident. Ryan in his turn gave a ghoulish account of the attack on Leon Trotsky, highlighting that the assassin's ice axe penetrated three inches into his brain. I needed another margarita before retiring to bed.

I picked up again with Amy this afternoon at the Museo La Venta in Villahermosa. In addition to the colossal three-dimensional Olmec heads, there are other intriguing carved altars. Amy was alone at Altar Four.

'These statues remind me of Easter Island,' I said.

'You've been there?'

'Twice.' There was silence and I wondered what to say next.

'This one is very disturbing,' she said. 'The figure of a tyrant, like a powerful bird, with his bound and helpless captive.'

'How do you know it's a "he"?'

She just gave me a strange look. Rather withering I felt.

'You know, Amy, its thirty-five years since I last saw you…' I began.

'I have a poor memory, Jeremy, and I don't care to think too much about the past.'

'I've never forgotten you,' I said. ' And I've never married you know.'

'Pity,' she said.

'How about you?'

'I'd rather not talk about my personal life.'

And she moved away. Odd. I wonder if she's married and in an unhappy relationship.

I looked for her friend, wondering if I might get a sense from her of what Amy's position is, but the pair of them appeared to have left the sculpture park.

This morning's route, to San Cristobal in the Chiapas Mountains, was interrupted by hijack attempts as the guidebook had warned it might be. Periodically the minibus was stopped by the presence of a thick rope held across the road, manned by vigilantes who demanded cash before they would open the route. The guide was apologetic to us, but I felt he was weak in dealing with the bandits. On the second occasion I left my seat and descended to accost the local robbers. I think they were impressed by my clearly authoritative appearance, and the formal diplomatic badge which I hurriedly dug out of my man-bag. Obviously the badge was irrelevant, but it did the trick and we were waved on. Thereafter Guillermo called for my assistance on each subsequent occasion, resulting in admiring glances from Marjorie and other members of the group, though disappointingly little reaction from Amy.

It is already day eight, going into day nine (as it is after midnight). It has been a momentous day.

We spent the late morning and early afternoon at the town of San Juan Chamula, about ten kilometres from San Cristobal. The population of the town is indigenous Tzotzil people and it is a quirky place with its own customs, governance and laws. In the main square, in front of the church of St Juan Bautista, we witnessed a violent altercation and an arrest. The arrested man was dragged off to an open prison on one side of the square – I say open, because the prison cell is open for the public to see, the humiliation being part of the punishment. Guillermo advised us that the man had an obsessional interest in his neighbour's wife and this had resulted in the confrontation. It sounded like a case of stalking, so that is clearly not just a western problem!

Entering the candle-lit church felt like stepping into a different world, after the heat of the square and the tension of the fight. The floor was covered in pine needles, bringing a strong aroma which mixed with the greasy smoke from thousands of lit candles, presumably there as votive offerings. There were no seats and people were sprawled across the floor, praying and chanting. Something of the scene took me back to my Catholic upbringing with strong memories of the confirmation process and its rituals. Although I abandoned my Catholic faith long ago, the impact of that two-year preparation period lives on, not least in the people I met during those otherwise interminable religious education classes.

As I was contemplating this echo from my past, I saw Amy kneel to the floor and apparently engage in prayer. Her friend, Rebecca, was strolling around the church evidently less impressed by the sense of the sacred. I approached Amy and knelt near to her. When she opened her eyes I spoke, quietly and with respect.

'Are you still a Catholic, Amy?' I asked.

'What do you mean?' she replied.

'Remember those deadly confirmation classes, and how we talked about them?' Amy was silent. 'The only thing that made them bearable was meeting you.' She started scrambling to her feet and I gently squeezed her arm and said, 'We must talk.' She looked round, but she sank back on her knees. I was able to be heartfelt.

'I used to lie awake, drowning from the pleasure of our trysts, remembering every detail. The time between our meetings was almost unbearable. Being with you alone, in the park, in the woods, those intimate meetings. I've never forgotten them. I've thought about you a lot. Wondered why we stopped seeing each other. Remember your confirmation name, Julia' – she looked quizzically at me for a moment – 'and me being confirmed as Joseph, the faithful one, the one who suffered, and not just from the confirmation slap. I've been posted all over the world, but never settled anywhere, always remembering our relationship. And now I've found you again, after all this time.'

Now she stood.

'I think you are mistaken,' she said, in a hoarse voice that was unlike her natural intonation. She was clearly emotional. From the corner of my eye I could see Rebecca approaching. Amy seemed to fall into her arms and there were sounds of sobbing. She feels the same as me, I thought. The moment was spoiled by a shriek, and as we all turned a wizened, elderly lady in front of us cut the throat of a chicken and squeezed the blood onto the needle strewn floor.

After that I felt impeded from a further dialogue with Amy. I considered we would have a more relaxed opportunity to engage during the theatrical performance that was part of the itinerary in the evening.

It was satirical comedy theatre presented in English and clearly intended for the tourists. The main act was the Mustachio Brothers who claimed to be Chilean and to have originally come to Mexico to go to the dentists. The dentist asked why they'd travelled to Mexico to have their teeth checked.

'Because we can't open our mouths in Chile,' they said.

It was hilarious stuff and a great poke at regimes that prevent people from expressing themselves. I enjoyed it, even without Amy, who it appeared had gone to bed early with a headache.

'She needs to be left alone,' said Rebecca, in rather an aggressive way when I asked where Amy was.

There were complimentary drinks which perhaps made everyone more relaxed. I don't like Rebecca though. Clive was on good form, suggesting that the indigenous population of Chamula should be forced to comply with national laws –

'You can't have people running their own affairs like that,' he said. 'It brings chaos, anarchy.'

I thought about my experiences in various African states, but forbore to put Clive in his place. Jemima said it was a shame that the man had gone to prison for being in love. Between Marjorie and J and J, I was bludgeoned by a constant diatribe of perceptions. Marjorie claimed to have been kept awake all night by a parrot and a series of pyrotechnic bangs. I had an intense headache by the time we left the theatre, when I just needed quiet to plan my next approach to Amy. The friend Rebecca was getting in the way.

Then on the way back to the hotel, whilst striving to keep away from Marjorie, I walked smack into a road sign. I didn't think it was a problem but when I shook my head, in response to concerned questions, I apparently splattered the rest of the group with blood. So, I have spent the last two hours with a private doctor having my head stitched. If that wasn't unpleasant enough, Marjorie insisted on accompanying me, 'so you wouldn't be on your own.' Being on my own was exactly what I wanted. The doctor even asked, in broken English, if she was my wife! Fat chance. However, I'm not going to let this spoil tomorrow's visit to Calakmul.

I did not sleep well last night. Hallucinatory half dreams that in the madness of the night seemed plausible. I was in a church with Amy, or was she now Julia? We were alone. It was like a game. She was moving fast, jockeying between the rows of pews, avoiding being caught. I was pursuing, excited, lusty, feeling that this was it, this was the moment. I was carrying a long, lit candle, but just as I got close to her the candle would blow out and I'd have to stop and light it again, the building pressure in my groin getting more and more intense.

Finally, I cornered her, in a dark alcove which was more like a castle than a church. For some reason she was wearing a gown now, with a hood like a monk. I couldn't see her face. As I drew near and smiled invitingly at her, she turned, and wrenched a halberd from the wall of the castle. Everything transformed in that moment, as she swung the weapon at me and her hood fell back to reveal her grimacing face. As my head was sliced away I was just conscious that I was not looking into the face of Amy, but that of my nemesis from the tour group – it was Marjorie. I struggled into consciousness with my hands round my neck, striving to stem the flow of blood from my cut throat. There was blood on my hands I could feel it, sticky and odorous.

When I woke up fully this morning there was blood on my pillow. I can't find another head wound, it must have been a nose bleed in the night. I am bleeding for Amy.

Let's see what today brings.

Customer feedback reports to the Méjico Travel Company

We are still awaiting your compensation offer. Administration of the claim has been very slow. Not only was the tour cut short as a result of the incident at Calakmul, but the entire Yucatan section of the holiday was compromised owing to the bizarre and unpleasant behaviour of one member of the group. Whilst we approve of the company's policy to be open in its promotion, we feel that the guide should have taken steps earlier to deal with the issues reported.

This holiday was planned as a special celebration for my girlfriend and myself. However, we felt uncomfortable from the beginning of the tour from Cancun, and this irritation was enhanced at Izamal, where it seemed that the person concerned was intrusively following us in an attempt to strike up some kind of relationship. We had to instruct our local guide to vary the tour itinerary in order to escape what appeared to be a peculiar pursuit on a horse and cart.

It was impossible to avoid this person at Uxmal and Villahermosa, where he quite clearly followed me as I explored the ruins and the artwork at La Venta on my own – a couple do not always want to stay together. It was clear that our guide perceived this stalking as some kind of huge joke.

Before the incident at Calakmul, the attentions came to a head at Chamula, where this person made wild suggestions, claiming we knew each other, intimately, from the past. This was distressing to me as a gay woman, especially as I am in a relatively new relationship. Once again the guide was unhelpful, actually asking if I wanted him placed in the town prison. By this time I was starting to fear that the man might become aggressive, his accident in San Cristobal reinforcing the unpredictability of his behaviour. Other members of the group seemed disinclined to listen to my concerns.

Both my friend and I were anxious about the trip to Calakmul.

With a fifty-kilometre private road through the jungle to reach the site, we were worried about the isolation of the place and how Mr X might behave, given his increasing intrusiveness.

Calakmul is an extraordinary Mayan site and should have been the highlight of our Yucatan tour. In the event we spent much of the time there playing what seemed to be a dangerous game of hide and seek. We stayed close together as a couple and also tried to remain in proximity to other members of the tour group. The guide left us at the entrance, providing no support or comfort. The huge scope of the site, and the encroaching jungle, coupled with the small number of visitors (I think our group were the only people on site at the time) made it increasingly difficult to move freely around and to experience the full extent of the ruins, whilst keeping a check on where the other people from the group were at any one time.

Towards the end of the afternoon we climbed the open stairway that ascends structure seven, with the intention to reach the three-chambered temple at the summit. My friend paused to take in the view, and as none of our tour group appeared to be on the pyramid I climbed onwards and entered the temple.

Mr X was sitting on a stone wall, inside the temple, wearing a mask that was presumably a replica he had bought elsewhere on the tour. I stood absolutely still, and called for Becky. He slowly took off the mask and it was apparent that he was experiencing some kind of fit. He was trying to speak, to communicate, his lips were moving and opening, but no words were coming from his mouth, just sounds and a distressing struggle to articulate. He looked panicked. Becky joined me and we both stood at the summit of the pyramid and called for help. We were joined on structure seven by other members of the group, including Isabelle, who is a nurse, and who identified that Mr X was experiencing a stroke.

It was many hours before formal medical help arrived, presumably that was arranged by the guide, and we ended up in temporary accommodation that night in Xpujil. The drive to Tulum the next day was delayed and no one in the group had the heart to go sightseeing. In effect our tour ended on that day in Calakmul, and the mood thereafter, and on our return journey to the UK, was restrained. We were given little information about the health of Mr X and I have no idea whether he recovered or not.

Amy Dickinson

This was a sadly dysfunctional tour. Certain members of the party seemed determined to undermine others, and to circulate unpleasant stories. Jeremy Johnson was not shown due respect for someone who has been in a senior diplomatic position. Not only that, he is knowledgeable about Mayan culture, and could correct the appointed guide on a number of matters. There was distressingly little interest in his health after he was taken ill at Calakmul, with party members more interested in the compensation they might receive for interruption of their holiday. I am glad to say that I have been to see Jeremy since his repatriation to England. He is sadly still unable to communicate verbally, but otherwise he is stable, albeit with some mobility issues. It is fortunate that he had taken early retirement and has sufficient resources to manage.

I will continue to visit him, and take care of him. It is an honour to support someone that I first met many years ago in church, and have always admired.

Marjorie Roberts

THIRTY A DAY

'I F YOU SAY TWENTY, YOU really mean thirty a day.'

There was raucous laughter. For the boy it was like watching and hearing cartoon characters – they seemed like gross, cut-out figures, ritualised in their thoughtless cruelty and unblinking ignorance. Even his mother, who had claimed 'twenty'. Her son cocked his head from the smell of vaporub and of the sofa upholstery where he'd been lying with a blanket cover to ward his asthmatic, chesty cold. The cartoon adults, the circle of friends, were smirking and gesticulating through the haze of tobacco smoke, smug in their nicotine-induced Sunday complacency, worlds away from understanding or empathising with childhood extremities of fear. But were cartoons not meant for children?

Thirty a day is worse than twenty, he thought, and silently cried into the abrasive red covering of the posh settee, a Sunday-preserved seat which had a solemn, upright posture, worthy and uncomfortable. He felt as constrained on his temporary sickbed as his chest felt constricted, his breath struggling overtime to gasp air into impoverished lungs.

Then the Sunday teapot was accidentally kicked over on the admired, pale-grey carpet, and the howling laughter stopped. Once the initial shock and chaotic call to action had subsided, only the huge brown stain was left, clear of tea leaves but nevertheless raw and visible despite the frantic scrubbing.

'You'll have to cover it with a hearth rug,' they mused. And so she did.

But from time to time, over the coming months, the boy would secretly lift that hearth rug and inspect the hidden stain, the malignant residue permeating the fibres, a never-fading mark. Lifting the hearth rug became a secret addiction, like taking down one huge volume of the Encyclopaedia Britannica to sniff the sanitised paper and read the incomprehensible description of carcinomas, whilst the television blurted cigarette advertisements in the background. It fed into the images he saw as he lay awake at night, as he watched for the frightening animations that he thought would come alive to terrorise him. Don't close your eyes, or go to sleep, or you'll be got.

It was only a few months after the teapot incident, that a queue of scared children, all carrying excuses, tentatively handed notes to a slight but formidable Grey Lady with sharp eyes. Grey Lady was accompanied by Grey Lady's assistant and both were uniformed in chill. Sharp eyes read the boy's note,

'What's the matter with your mother?' she pierced.

'She's got an ulcer.'

Satisfied grunt. But he knew there was something wrong. There was an unspoken and alarming conversation taking place, the messages passing between Grey Lady and her assistant as if in code. He accepted what he was told, but always knowing deep inside, in the place where he had an enquiring mind, and an older inner knowledge, that this was to do with matters unmentionable. It was about scary, life changing and end-of-the-world-as-you-know-it stuff. His asthma was better, but his world had changed overnight.

His night-time fears had manifested in real time. The uniforms retreated, leaving him with a new burden of anxiety.

The cancer ward only allowed children to visit on Sunday afternoons, and then for a prescribed two hours. So an endless list of stranger families, with different rituals and rules, provided a rota of weekday and weekend meals and hostelry, dispensing hygienic care to a silent, grieving only child of an only parent – a child too scared (force-fed on politeness) to question unexplained routines and diets, dissimilar table manners and unfamiliar preferences. Tears would embarrass the host, and in any case suppurated anxieties were to be dismissed as over-imagination, a foolish fearfulness to be mocked in behind-hands group whispers.. The asthma too was apparently hysteria, but the value of care in the community overrode the anxieties of overburdened social care.

The boy lived for letters and motherly gifts from the scrubbed isolation of the hospital fortress. The staff there were clones, protective of their knowledge and antiseptic in righteousness. Smoking was not allowed, but the patients smoked anyway, and not just in the day room (for those who could reach it). He knew this, because there was that faint lingering smell, in the air and on bedclothes, and the yellow staining of the walls and ceilings betrayed the religion.
'After all, if you're going to die…,' he heard someone say.
And he continued to be battered by messages and images that focused and reinforced his terror. He could not ignore any reference, however oblique: the colour supplement, abandoned on a front seat of the double decker bus amidst the debris of cigarette ends, featured an interview with a well-known Hollywood actor dying as a result of his smoking habit; a stark diagram taped to the wall of the dentists' waiting room illustrated the signs that indicate

malignancy, including retracted upper lip. The boy added to his addiction and started to visit the triptych mirror in the spare room, looking for telltale signs of retraction. But no-one spoke to him directly. No-one mentioned the dread word in relation to him or his mother. According to the cartoon friends, she would soon be returning home.

Each week a relative, or sometimes a godparent, would appear and grudgingly stay over for a night or two so that he could be at home. They would complain about the discomfort of the spare bed, but not be brave enough to lie in the mother's imprint. Night after night, when this happened, the boy would wakefully stare at the model Coldstream Guard and coronation coach on the narrow ledge above his bedroom window, fearful in this small refuge that was also a prison. He started to displace the original fear of animated monsters with fear of his mother's death, and then of his own. In order to cope, he silently built an immunity to love.

He was increasingly trapped in a world that would not allow recognition of threat or change, and yet in which change was a constant threat and fear. He managed by reading only familiar books, grasping the security of any routine that was available, and by learning to believe that truth was simple, black and white in its solutions. Nothing could challenge this contradictory stability. But still the fear would not go away. Rather the fear began to grow, and it was monstrous. It mushroomed from his core, like ugly, uncontrollable rising yeast, and like the expanding growths he had seen at school in an overflowing petri dish. It was as if the fear was stretching his skin, expanding it remorselessly to the point of cracking, bursting open. The fear led to uncontrollable spasms in his neck and to twitches below his eyes, revealing his inner turmoil and raising his metabolism to a sprint.

But no one noticed.

With practice, the boy hid his tension. There was only one

option and he knew it was to stop caring. He must stop loving, otherwise it was too unbearable. The decision was made. Once committed it was like delivery of a corporate strategy. A subtle, internal process commenced, and there was an inevitability that it would be fulfilled. This was not immediate; not a change in a "now you do, now you don't," way; but gradually the transformation would take place, and would be completed.

So, increasingly the horror stories the boy heard from the cancer ward were numbed by the crusting of his exterior and inner feelings. The haemorrhage that afflicted his mother's neighbour was a particularly vivid example. He imagined the nightmarish elements as an animation that could simply be switched off. The catalogue of newly missing patients, highlighted by his weekly hospital visit, was unemotionally noted, as was the careful exchange of beds that led those who were closest to their demise to be at the near end of the ward. Was this to make it easier to wheel away the corpse, he wondered? He noted his mother's position in the room, midway. He reckoned she had six weeks.

Sometimes, whilst he visited the hospital, the vending trolley would weave its way through the ward, pushed and pulled by a voluminous Black trolley dolly who emerged from the special, unvisited side ward, like a character in *Tom and Jerry*. But there were no chases, no flattened porter, just the unintelligible and strident hawking as the frugally filled trolley dished its wares around the ward, wares that included Cadets No. 1 and even Capstan Full Strength for the bravest. The score to be achieved was perhaps not thirty a day, but still a forgettable number that could be smoked.

One Sunday afternoon, with his mother asleep, he approached the trolley and hesitantly purchased a packet of twenty. As he paid for the cigarettes he was unsure whether this was a gift for his mother, his way of saying he understood, or perhaps in a more sinister sense, a way of shrugging off his old concerns. Or was this going to be his secret – his initiation into the club, that adult world of tough and brutal cynicism, the wiping away of memories of childhood fears and terror. The cartoon vendor, assuming the purchase was for his mother, delightedly gave him his change, calling him her *little man*.

On the bus back home he studied the packet, opened the cardboard drawer and removed the slither of intoxicating silver paper. The packet burnt a hole in his pocket as he walked the quarter mile from the bus stop. His godmother was waiting for him. He saw her swift movement in the front window as he approached the house – she had been waiting.

'Where've you been?' she said, 'I'm waiting to go out. It's Bingo night down at the church hall. You'll be alright till I get back. There's food for you in the oven.'

There was a full ashtray on the hearth, smoke still curling from the hastily stubbed cigarette.

'How many a day?' he asked her.

'What are you talking about?'

'How many a day do you smoke?'

'None of your business,' she replied. 'Why do you want to know?'

He shrugged. 'I bet it's thirty.'

'No,' she said. 'Never more than twenty.'

'Is twenty safe?' he asked.

'Get on with you,' she said. 'Cigarettes don't do you any harm. Keep you sane, that's what they do.'

At which she gathered up a fresh packet, put on her coat and left the house. Silence.

The boy was left alone. He sighed and went into the kitchen. Opening the oven door produced a wave of thick smoke that made him choke as the heat seared his lungs. The food was unappetising.

He went into the front room. There was still a thin trail of smoke from the ash tray. He lay down on the red settee in his outdoor shoes and stared at the hearth rug. Then he stood and rolled the rug back to expose the ugly brown stain, the carpet fibres separated and damaged by the alien substance they had absorbed and that was now embedded. He placed the new packet of cigarettes on the settee, moved the ashtray next to them and fetched matches from the kitchen. Then he pulled down Volume 3 of the Encyclopaedia and opened it at the page for carcinomas. He lay back on the settee and lit a cigarette. The taste was unpleasant, and when he sucked in he felt a searing heat in his lungs, just as when he'd opened the oven door. He lay the smouldering cigarette, tentatively, on the page of the Encyclopaedia. A brown, yellow stain started to form on the thin paper. Then he used the bright end of the cigarette to burn a hole, right through the *O* in carcinoma. By the time the cigarette was ready to stub out there was a pattern of circles with brown edges, like miniature bullet holes criss-crossing the paper.

Then he leant over from the edge of the settee, and with his next cigarette he tested burning a hole in the stain on the carpet. Could he burn away the brown stain? It took some experimentation. After a while he found that he could burn the brown fibres out, but that there was a still a light brown base underlying the damaged carpet. By now caution had ceased and he was sucking in the cigarette smoke like a hardened addict, pulling beyond the early coughing fits to an overwhelming sense of dizziness and nausea. Despite the nausea he felt better, powerful, like he was an adult in the adult world. He had left the cartoons behind. Or had he joined them?

Rolling from the sofa the boy managed to crawl to the stairs, and to slowly climb upwards. Reaching the landing, where in the recent past he would have expected to imagine disfigured, animated creatures emerging from each hidden doorway or alcove, he was scarily fear-free. He went into his mother's bedroom and lay down on the bed. For once he did not need to glue himself facing the door, eyes unblinking, ready to cope with, or respond to, the appearance of any terrifying two-dimensional monsters..

He fell asleep and dreamed about the little boy and his mother in that special *Looney Tunes* cartoon. He smelt the bully's cigar and coughed his smoke, as the world went round and round and that song played in his head:

You'll smoke until you start to bake.

In her bed at the near end of the cancer ward the boy's mother was the subject of frenzied, whispered attention. She saw the medical staff clustered and deep in animated conversation. She didn't know why, but she remembered what it had been like as a child to feel helpless out-of-control fear, fear that she could do nothing to ease. She wished her son was there with her.

At least he was safely in their home, with his godmother to look after him. She would buy him something special from the vending trolley on Sunday. She still didn't understand why he had bought her cigarettes when she was asleep. Perhaps he would bring them this time.

She was down to ten a day now, and planned to give up when she left hospital.

'That's all folks,' the boy heard, in his dreamless sleep.

3250

TODAY I AM ONE THOUSAND years old.

I intend to visit Hannah, back in the year 2000, on the day of her birthday.

Hannah feels my presence. She sits straight up in bed, alert, and she looks directly at me. She can't see me, but I wonder if she has an image of me, of the real Miranda. I wish I could communicate with her. At first she tenses, feeling that I am there, but as she calms her fear I stay and watch over her, as if I'm a carer tending to someone who is sick. She relaxes in bed. This is timeless for me. I want to stroke her dark, wavy hair and to feel the texture of her clear, pale skin. I want to learn to smell and to taste her body, but these are not senses that I can enjoy.

In the year 2000 Hannah is pure. It is her birthday and she is in no hurry to rise. She doesn't know that in five years' time she will tape a clear, airtight bag over her head and will inhale deadly gas, gasping this into her system, breathing in its poison until her body dies. I have watched that scene, more than once, but I cannot intervene. Even during those moments Hannah seems to know I am there. She struggles, but I cannot relieve her suffering. Nor can I punish those responsible.

But for now, Hannah sits in front of the triptych looking glass in her room. She is examining her profile. It is as if she is looking for another person, trying to find a different identity in the multiple images she can see. Is she looking for me? Does she think she can see me? When she cut out those letters, and placed them on a table, in a circle, and begged the glass to tell her who was present, it must have been her own mind that encouraged the glass to spell my name – M-I-R-A-N-D-A. We of the thirty-third century are not able to interact with the past. That is neither permissible nor possible. We cannot alter the past. We can observe and reflect, but we cannot participate. To these people, living in the so-called Age of Digital Information, our visits are ethereal. Only some of them register a fleeting sense of our presence. For those who can feel us we are ghosts to them. Phantoms. They believe in us if they will.

We who have conquered death, and the need for love, can observe, and can celebrate the progress that precludes us from the suffering that Hannah experiences. Her story unfolds for me. I have watched her many times. I know Hannah intimately. I have seen all her moods, her private musings and her moments of despair. I have observed how her life, and death, play out. I have seen her confusion over the adoration that she is given by another in her present life, not knowing how to respond to the person involved; not knowing if she wants to respond to this person. Maybe she is wondering now about the spirit that she can feel, the "ghost" that she is aware of, as I circle around her space. I am her guardian angel. She comes back to her looking glass and then reverts to the cut-out letters. Asking for information. Asking for help.

But I am not able to respond to her request. The response is not mine. Hannah takes from the talking board only what her mind is able to invent. It is all wrong. It is fake. I cannot reach her to explain, to influence her. I can only be registered as a fleeting moment of disturbance, an airy spirit.

The talking board continues to invite her to speak with "Miranda". The messages suggest she is communicating with someone long gone. This Miranda says she cares for Hannah, is her guide, and gives advice. Miranda tells Hannah to close down the relationship with the man, the relationship that she has developed, that is confusing for her.

Hannah is coming back often to the talking board. Now she has stopped registering my presence. Or maybe she has become used to it. She is obsessed with this "other" Miranda, this supposed spirit from the past.

I should like to tell Hannah about life where I come from. We have endless time in 3250. We are timeless. Our bodies are forever replaceable. We are small in number, simply those who received the gift of eternal life when the mechanisms of human evolution and regeneration ceased.

We do not have conflict in 3250; there is no need. Why would we? Hannah would recognise the natural world that we have around us, though nature itself has been tamed. She would recognise the flora and fauna in our special reservations. This is a carefully controlled world, harmonious. However, we are continuously alert, aware to the possibility of visitors that may arrive from a different cosmos. This is our only fear, our anticipation of an Armageddon. But there is no evidence of any kind to suggest that these visitors exist, or that they are on their way to challenge us. We can therefore concentrate on our primary task, our research. Our research involves revisiting and learning from past epochs. We learnt how to reach back and to have an observational presence in previous periods of time. This access provides opportunities for knowledge.

The great challenge remains the twenty-first century, the Age of Digital Information, from which virtually nothing survives. Even the buildings are mostly gone. This was a dark, destructive period, out of which little was archived, and as a consequence many of us return here to observe it at first hand, and to conduct research that will enable us to share more detail of that momentous Age. It helps us to understand our own trajectory of progress. Change has led us to our current world order, our societal structure, constructed for survival and for our safety. We are the beneficiaries. The chosen. We live in a world of order, and of calm.

Unlike Hannah.

I met Hannah for the first time in her year 2000. I have not journeyed further back to meet her prior to that birthday, as that first encounter is sacred to my contact with her. I watched her, and was present with her, until the day she took her life. That was five years of her time, her life. For me it is moments in eternity. I have time to invest. I like looking at her body. I like hearing her laugh, watching her move, especially when she is carefree, before the man and the talking table intervene. It is a pleasure to see Hannah prepare herself for an evening of leisure. Her clothes are chosen with such appreciation. We do not need these things in 3250.

I do not comprehend the concept of suicide. Perhaps it existed because the world of the twenty-first century was confused and chaotic. I try to understand, to unpick the route that Hannah followed. She shared my birth date. Five birthdays I shared with her. The last, though, was not pleasant.

When the man became part of her life, things changed. It spoilt everything. He made new demands on her, required responses of her. He touched her. I know she didn't want him, but he seemed insistent, forceful. Hannah pretended that she wanted this man, but I observed that she increasingly locked herself away, taking out those cut-out letters and the moving glass. She was more and more often speaking to that person through the talking board, that person she believed existed; that person her mind had constructed, and to whom she chose to give my name. She wanted to know how this Miranda had died. How old she had been when that happened, whether she had been in love. It was as if she was in a relationship with that person. That person from the past. A person who seemed to haunt her, to need her and to want to live through her. Hannah was being consumed.

The man also became increasingly attentive. He would expect to see her at different times. He brought gifts. He wanted to share her bed, and sometimes she let him. It was with dismay that I saw her comply. This was an attack on her purity. She was becoming damaged.

That night of the final birthday party, I watched her get ready. She had a long bath. It seemed as if she was calm in my presence, and as if the other Miranda was not disturbing her. She looked in the triptych mirror to fasten those earrings, long, dangly, sparkling earrings. He had given them to her. They framed her pale face. Flawless. Yet she frowned in the mirror.

Now it was as if she knew that someone was watching her. Did she think it was the other? The fake Miranda from her talking board? I wanted to explain it was me, but that is not possible. I cannot communicate. Her composure had cracked. She became restless, clumsy, knocked her chair over, fell against the dressing table; the mirror rocked and fell. When she stood the triptych up, she saw that the glass was broken. Hannah was distraught. She took it as an omen, rushed to the letters that she had avoided using that day. Miranda was telling her she must die, must join her, so they could be together. Hannah threw down the talking table glass and wept.

Then the man came. He accused her. She had no right to cry. It was her birthday. She must celebrate. Come to the party. They would have a great time. People would be there to see her.

She left with the man, but she kept looking around her, as if she was being followed. I watched, carefully. I don't think she wanted the man at her side.

At the party I think she was always hoping to escape his presence. He would slip his arm through hers, but she would unhook it, she was uneasy. People commented, asked if she was alright. She was in distress, I could see. Drinking a lot. It was her birthday. It was mine as well, of course. At the party she was introduced to new people, to some friends of the man. She asked one if their name was Miranda. The man was angry. He told her she had an obsession, that she needed help. He could not carry on, he said. He was shouting. I could not protect her. He is responsible. She left.

When she gets back to where she lives, she does not return to the talking board. I watch her take out the canister of gas, the canister that she had purchased for this one special occasion, whenever that might come. She places an envelope on her dressing table. I have not seen her write the note. I can't find that moment. Why can't I find that moment? She must have written it one night in the dark, secretly. Her only secret from me. Was that deliberate?

It is all ready, all planned ahead, waiting for the right moment. She drinks some wine, and then she places the death mask over her head, pumps the gas and sucks deeply to draw the poison into her. She is gasping, her face is distorted, and then she sleeps. I can watch no more.

I don't understand why I keep returning to Hannah. There is much to keep me in my own time and so much else to research. It is as if I cherish a hope that each time I return the outcome may be different. Perhaps she will not take her own life, maybe she will be more aware of my presence, of the real Miranda, instead of this fake, talking-table persona that Hannah has increasingly come to listen to. But I know I cannot change the past. It is not possible. My Hannah must die.

It is the year 3250 and I am one thousand years old. I will have a party. What a party. Not like the party that Hannah experienced, that day when she opened the gas canister, prepared the face mask, and took her life. Now I have decided that I will, after all, visit the time after Hannah's death. I will find out whether those responsible were made to suffer. Whether the man was made to suffer. I hope so.

This is my treat for my thousand-year birthday.

I am in a room, and it is another party. A different party. It is a death party. They are all sombre. There are many people there that I know from Hannah's life. He is there. The man, I mean. The man that caused Hannah grief, and that led her to determine to end her life. He is very sad, though, and he is being comforted, not rebuked. There are pictures of her life, moving pictures. People are whispering. They say she had an illness; that she was spooked, obsessional; that this is why she became ill and took her life; that the man had been a comfort, had done everything he could. The man is shown her letter. The letter she left when she decided to end her life. It was in the envelope on her dressing table, by the cracked triptych. He reads it and I stand close. He is not aware of me. No-one is aware of me in that room. None of them can feel me. This letter is burnt now into my knowledge.

When you find me, I will have gone to another place to find peace. I am invaded and I cannot escape. I am being taken over. I hear the voice, feel the presence, and this fills all my waking moments. It is impossible to bear. I am no longer me. I have no identity. I am losing my mind to Miranda. She is ever present. I have to get away. Hannah

I go back to the year 2000. I watch Hannah once more, when she is perfect, carefree. I like this year. Where better to spend the rest of my birthday.

I love her.

I love her and she will never know. I love her and I want to live in the twenty-first century.

I love her and I want to live in confusion and chaos.

I want to know what it is like to die.

HOUSE CLEARANCE

EST VIEW. STRANGE NAME. THERE was no view. The charged stillness of the house enveloped me even as I stepped onto the open wooden porch. It was late afternoon in early autumn. Piles of rotting leaves disguised the intricate floor tiling, and there was a shudder as the front door swung open to reveal evidence of activity abruptly abandoned. It was as if the occupants had simply got up and walked out, in response to some catastrophic emergency.

It was a time-warp. A spectacle case lay open on the wooden hall stand, glasses nearby, one arm bent back and the lens harbouring cracked glass. There was a harsh, almost malevolent ticking from an imposing grandfather clock, partly visible on the landing as I shifted my gaze to the wide stairway and polished wooden balustrade. The hall walls and rise above the stairs were busily decorated with pictures and trophies, including a broken deer skull and antlers, out of context in an early Edwardian property – who had furnished and decorated this dark, sombre space?

Clocks everywhere. In the rear dining room, a huge circular oak table, and a decrepit piano with yellow sunken keys, like the worn stone steps of a medieval castle. Drawers which opened to reveal war medals carelessly thrown in alongside bottle tops, broken pocket watches and gaily decorated matchbooks. A grotesque carved statuette on the mantel, neighboured by old cigarette and pastille tins. I opened one; it was stuffed with what I took to be pubic hair. A love memento? Or something more sinister? I didn't dare open any more.

The rear breakfast room was a little more homely, with an old-style radio and a table covered in a thick, velvet tablecloth that felt inviting to the touch. A tabloid paper was open with a half-completed crossword, pen thrown carelessly to one side as the occupant had apparently negotiated their escape. A pools coupon. Door in the corner, opened with a shove to reveal damaged red-brick steps down to a cellar pantry, at least six inches deep in filthy water. A small rear kitchen beyond the breakfast room.

I retraced my steps to the front room where there was a little more light and less of a chill. A beautiful French skeleton clock sat in a broken glass dome, held together by peeling sellotape. A book of savings stamps was open on an antique side table, and felt curiously out of place. Someone had been saving for a cheap consumer gift, carefully licking the stamps and pressing them into the book on a seventeenth-century table that was badly scratched. A cake stand in the corner of the room. How many cakes had been eaten from it during afternoon tea, and by whom? When did it last host a Victoria Sponge?

I am a house clearance operative.

I am familiar with neglect, with mould and decay. I have seen ruined interiors defiled by animals and slovenly people, but this house spooked me. It combined the ambience of a museum with that of a ghost train. It had a strong presence, a sense that pulling away just one minute might spring the house and its occupants back into life, in whatever tragedy they were playing out. I wondered why my customer, Maxwell, would not meet me in this strange place. Instead, he had passed me the keys, indicating he wanted total clearance and an empty property. He hardly spoke.

Surely he might have wanted to explore some of the objects here, some of the closed secrets that this house might reveal. I understood it had been a family home. Would that not mean special memories, even family heirlooms? It was a treasure trove and a junk shop intertwined and dissolved together in a pot-pourri of poignant artefacts, textures, colours and smells.

Maxwell himself must have been here, and recently; there was no accumulated post and the grandfather clock was ticking.

Upstairs felt cold and looked damp. Five bedrooms. A small box room, perhaps the servant quarters a hundred years ago. The long case clock on the landing, disturbing and dominating the stillness. A stunning clock face, personalised with the maker's name, with Roman numerals and gold decorative features. I was tempted into turning the little brass key to peer at the pendulum. The inside of the case was unexpectedly covered in ink drawings, many were caricatures, like a series of stories. These were additions, not part of the original clock case. Were they drawn by someone in the family? Weird.

Bathroom quaint. No modernisation here. This had been the home of an elderly person. Maxwell's father? Grandfather?

In one bedroom an old writing box, antique, an ancient bed-warmer, and architectural drawings. Plans of a prison, Victorian judging by the date. Why were there plans for a Victorian prison strewn on a wicker laundry basket in a back bedroom at West View?

One room with wardrobes filled with women's clothes, musty old clothes, out of date clothes, looking as if they'd been there for years. A Girl Guide Leader uniform. In another room the smell of an elderly woman. How do I know that? Experience. Back on the landing an attic opening in the ceiling, just in front of the grandfather clock, the entrance clearly sealed, unused. At least there was no additional baggage there for clearance.

Ha. West View would soon be bustling at auction with those who know the value of a pastille tin and broken pocket watch. Good luck to them.

I made my escape, looking back at the box room window as I started my car, convinced I could see a watching face. A little boy?

West View had been left to itself, unoccupied for months. Maxwell had dutifully visited on a fortnightly basis; briefly dealing with the post, checking there had been no intruders, and ensuring that late frosts and subsequent thaw had not damaged water pipes or led to serious flooding in the damp, pre-Edwardian cellar.

Each time he visited he cautiously ventured upstairs. It was only to open the long case clock and swiftly rewind the pendulums, a mechanical action he performed like his father and grandfather before him, a task repeated, usually on a weekly basis, for a hundred years. Now it was fortnightly and still the clock had not stopped. Maxwell unerringly, but unwillingly, climbed the stairs and cranked the weights back up. He felt as if he had no choice, though he avoided focusing on the detailed ink drawings that decorated the interior. Out of habit he would also glance upwards and shudder, registering the cobwebs festooning the old attic entrance.

Sometimes, if he stayed awhile, he heard the clock jarringly announce the hour. It was an unpleasant, almost aggressive metallic chime, and always then he felt a nauseous wave of intense fear, disappointment and sadness, a muscle memory.

Meanwhile, Maxwell's father lay wrapped in a cocoon of coughing and confusion in the hospital dementia ward. By now it was late summer. He did not have dementia, but he could not return to the house. He lived out his last weeks between confused certainty he was at home and, in moments of clarity, angry uncertainty about his treatment at the hospital.

But the house lived on, in the father's temporary and then final absence. It had been the home where he had been a child, and where he had returned as a separated, middle aged, and then elderly man. Dying where he started. The house had changed little over those eighty or so years.

It was a place that was stuffed with an ancestry going back beyond Maxwell's father to his father before him. A place where no one dared make change, a place that hid many secrets.

Whilst undertaking a half-hearted attempt to sort through his father's possessions – the album of seaside postcards, the busy collection of cigarette cards, newspaper cuttings, the tins of ancient coins and fob watches, the mantle clocks and wrist watches, Maxwell came across the tiny diary. It was for a year that he remembered well, even though he had only been six years old. The year that he had lived at West View, whilst his parents attempted to sort out their messy marital life. It was his grandmother's diary.

With the aid of that diary he could now place a specific date and time on the incidents that were so alive in his emotional muscle memory.

He knew that the man climbing the rope had come first. For years he'd had nightmares about that moment – going upstairs at West View to cajole his grandfather down for supper. On the landing he'd seen legs ascending into the ceiling and through the hole into the attic he thought he'd seen a Chinaman climbing up a rope and scowling down at him. It was a recurring dream. He had backed into the clock before he turned and ran downstairs.

After that he recalled sitting with his grandmother in the

room by the kitchen. There was a fire in the grate. As usual she was engaged in her sewing and spoke little. He knew to be quiet. The doorbell rang. You could hear it clearly, echoing down the hall passageway. She had looked sharply at him and then rose to answer the door, taking an eternity to walk the long dark hallway. Maxwell got down from his chair and quietly reached up to open the door, a crack. At the end of the hall he could see the deer skull on the wall and his father, taking off his overcoat and hat, placing them on the coat stand. Not a word was spoken at first. Finally, his father said, 'this is a bad business.' Then he went upstairs and Maxwell's grandmother followed him slowly behind.

Even from the kitchen area Maxwell could hear the sharp ticking of the grandfather clock. He stood and waited for his father to reappear and to walk down the hall to see him, to hug him and to tell him he was loved and that everything was alright. To tell him that he could come home, did not need to stay in that dark, dead, chilling house any longer, could come away from the man climbing the rope. But, when his father did reappear, he came swiftly down the stairs, retrieved his hat and coat and left, without a single glance down the passage to where his son stood expectantly in the doorway, tears rolling down his face. The grandfather clock remorselessly chanted the hour as the front door slammed shut.

Maxwell had pushed the door shut once more and gone back to his seat, crying into the folds of the tablecloth, trying to hide his tears as his grandmother re-entered the room.

She sat down and picked up her sewing, a flickering look, from time to time, disturbing him. He stared back.

After a while she said, 'your grandfather has gone to a better place.' She paused. 'He was a good man, despite everything.' Then she added 'The man on the rope has gone now. You should forget him. It was a bad dream.'

The moment left an imprint. It determined the rest of his life.

He looked up and faced his grandmother's icy stare. She dropped her gaze and continued sewing. Maxwell kept his tension clenched in and remained dry eyed.

'We'll have chops for tea,' she said, and continued with her work. Nothing would be the same again. On another day he added his own ink drawing to the inside of the long case clock.

Sixty years later, Maxwell sat in the very place at the breakfast table where part of him had been frozen in perpetuity all those years before. The diary was on the table in front of him. He had read the short unsentimental entries with references to his grandfather's increasing ill health and depression, and his parents' disagreements. There was a strong sense of disapproval in the carefully constructed sentences. It was also clear that Maxwell had not been a welcome guest at West View. His grandfather's subsequent suicide, by hanging from a beam in the attic, was briefly and brutally referenced. No reference to Maxwell's misconception, his interpretation of a Chinaman. There was much repressed anger in the diary entries. The tolling of the grandfather clock interrupted his reverie.

Maxwell put the diary in his pocket, stood and opened the door, looking down the passageway to the front door. Above it, the deer skull stared back at him through sightless eyeholes. He still found it necessary to keep it in his vision as he walked along the passage, fearful it would come alive if he dropped his gaze. As always he stepped backwards up the stairs until the skull was out of sight.

He stopped in front of the grandfather clock, and opened it. This time he forced himself to look at the subversive ink drawings that littered the inside of the clock case. They were drawings that had frightened him as a child, not least because they seemed to multiply and develop every time he peeped inside the case. They were like caricature illustrations from a Victorian novel, telling stories. He did not know who had drawn them, or when, other than his own. He recognized faces in the drawings. But why, even now, were there new drawings he had not seen before? Maxwell furiously wound the pendulum to its maximum height. The clonk of the weights brought him back to himself.

In his father's bedroom, that had been his grandfather's before that, he inserted the delicate bureau key and clicked open the folding lid. The bureau was surprisingly ordered. His father's last will and testament had been written some years before. The instructions were clear. The property and all it contained had been left to his only son, Maxwell, provided he moved into the house and retained the contents. There was no specification as to what was meant by the contents, no inventory. Otherwise, the will stated, the property and everything in it were left to an obscure animal charity.

The bureau also held a large package wrapped in string, carefully tied. Maxwell sat on the bed and opened the package. The contents were architectural plans. They were the designs for a prison, a well-known prison, notorious now for its squalor and its isolation cells, and also for the flawed design that had maximised cost-saving above all else. The papers identified his grandfather's architectural business and his prison design. It was a business that Maxwell's father had inherited and briefly maintained until damning revelations made it impractical to preserve the legacy. The business was no more, but the prison...

Maxwell threw the plans onto the laundry basket and intuitively picked up the walking stick that his father had depended on in his last few years. He found himself hobbling along the landing, and clutching the stick he shook it in the direction of the attic entrance. Then he walked back down the shiny stairs, careful not to fall, as his father had done only a few months before. In the hallway he stopped, looked up at the deer skull, and with a strong swing of the stick smashed the skull where it hung.

Away from West View, Maxwell came to a decision.

He approached the nearest house clearance firm, and without seeking a quotation placed the operation in their hands. He instructed them to put the house contents up for auction, keeping nothing.

Six weeks later Maxwell returned to West View. He calmly walked upstairs, nonchalantly stepping into each room, looking and then closing the doors quietly behind him as he left. Everything had gone. In the room next to the kitchen there was no remnant of the table, the velvet cloth or the ancient radio. Standing there, the door slightly ajar, Maxwell put his hand in his pocket and recovered the little diary that his grandmother had kept.

He could still hear the deadly tick tock of the grandfather clock even after the clearance. With a last wave of antipathy the invisible clock struck violently again and again. Maxwell counted beyond a hundred before the rage died and the noise ceased, forever.

Maxwell walked briskly down the hall, opened the front door, stepped out and shut it for the last time. As an afterthought he took the diary from his pocket and posted it through the letterbox. Without looking back he stepped out of the drive and walked down the road to the High Street, where he would leave the keys with the selling estate agent.

He whistled softly to himself as he went.

Printed in Great Britain
by Amazon

17874430R00109